Broken

Appointments

Elaine Flowers

Published 2011 by
Hollygrove Publishing, Inc.
4100 West Eldorado Parkway
Suite 100-182
McKinney, Texas 75070
www.hollygrovepublishing.com

Cover designs by Cupcake Creative Studio
Editing by EBM Professional Services

13 Digit ISBN: 978-0984090488
10 Digit ISBN: 0984090487
Printed in the United States of America

Flowers, Elaine
Broken Appointments – First Edition

This book is dedicated to my mother,

Rosie Whiters Vesey

and my aunts, who are too numerous to name. For
fear that I may unintentionally omit one, if you are
my aunt please fill in the blank with your name here:

Aunt _____

Special thanks to Brian Smith at Hollygrove
Publishing for believing in me as a writer.
Thank you to the book clubs and readers who have
followed my work and have patiently awaited the release
of Broken Appointments.

Enjoy!

Broken

Appointments

Chapter 1 *Joyce Parker*

..just needed to be stirred up.

"Hmm... Joyce, your dressing looks different," Glory said, knowing for a fact I had not made the dressing.

"I made the dressing," Frannie spoke up, falling right into Glory's trap.

Glory scooped some dressing onto her plate. "Umm... What's wrong with it?"

"Ain't nothing wrong with my dressing."

"Looks as though you got a little carried away with the sage," Glory said. "It's green."

"It is not green!"

"This is definitely green," Glory said, staring at it.

"Well, you sure put some on your plate."

"I didn't want to be rude."

"Shut up, Glory," I said.

"What? I didn't say it wouldn't be tasty, I just said it was green."

"Well, what did you make?" Frannie asked Glory, looking around the table.

"Exactly what you see me making now—*my plate.*" Someone at the table snickered, but I wasn't exactly sure who.

Frannie was still huffing. "That's what I thought."

"Oh, don't act as if I can't cook," Glory said, knowing that no one would argue with that. She passed the dish to Wendell.

"Whether you can or can't, you didn't. *And that's my point.*"

A peaceful Thanksgiving with my family was obviously asking too much. Not only was a fight not surprising, it was expected. Sanita, my middle daughter that we affectionately called Sweetie, watched as her two sisters, Glory and Francine, verbally tore into each other. And I just thought, *It just wasn't a Parker gathering unless Frick and Frack were at each other's throats.*

I sat at the head of the large cherry wood table with my family surrounding me. To my right were my mother, Grandma Francine; Sweetie and her boys, Bryce and Anthony; my youngest daughter, Frannie, and her husband, Michael, along with their three children, Mikie, Brandon, and Ericka.

Glory and her boyfriend of the month, LaRone, were to my left. My widowed and childless sister, Jeanette, was on the other end of the table. Across from her were my son, Wendell and his daughter, Sydney.

Wendell plopped some dressing onto his plate, and then onto Sydney's. "Both uh' y'all shut up. Can't neither one of you cook."

"Where's the gravy?" Glory asked, looking at the liquid that sat in the gravy boat.

LaRone picked it up and handed it to her. "Here you go," he said, looking eager to ease the mounting tension between the two sisters. He looked amazed that no one seemed to be affected by the bickering.

Glory swirled the greasy goop around and then sat it back on the table. *"I know that ain't the gravy."*

The fuse had been reignited.

"I see you got your clown suit on today, Glo." Frannie picked up the gravy boat and spooned out the matter that had settled to the bottom. "...just needed to be stirred up." After pouring gravy on every morsel of food she had on her plate, she handed it to her husband, Michael, who hesitated and then poured a dab on his mashed potatoes.

"First of all—"

And here we go. Once someone had been "first-of-alled," it was officially a fight.

"You're the only one here without kids. *You* should've been the one helping Joyce with Thanksgiving dinner. It's just like a niggah to not do any of the work, but do all of the complaining." Frannie turned to secure Ericka's bib as she sat in her high chair.

Just as Glory was opening her mouth to rebut, Michael made his best attempt to hijack the conversation. "Hey man," he said to Wendell, "how is the school coming together up in Kansas City?"

I was relieved.

"It's going really well," Wendell replied. "Why don't you come up and see for yourself?"

"We should all go and check it out," I chimed in, happy to change the course of the conversation. After all, we did have a guest.

"Why don't you think about becoming an instructor?" Wendell asked me.

Wendell had recently started a cosmetology school in Kansas City that he was trying to get off the ground. He knew I'd been holding on to an instructor's license for years, but had never put it to any use. He'd been dropping hints for months about me returning to the classroom.

"I'm too old-fashioned for these young kids today. And I don't know if I have the patience." I got up and stood over my grandson, Anthony, piling more macaroni and cheese and turkey onto his plate because he liked to eat.

"Your experience is exactly what makes you so valuable. It's what's missing from this new generation of hairstylists. They don't want to hear about the basics like finger waves and roller placements. They just want to jump up and slap a ponytail on somebody and charge 'em eighty dollars."

"Hey, I spent fourteen hours behind the chair yesterday. Please tell me we are not getting ready to talk hair all day," Glory said.

"I know that's right. And I have to turn around and work again tomorrow," Sweetie added. "Pass me the rolls please, Aunt Jeanette."

"You're not hitting the mall with me and Glo tomorrow?" Frannie asked.

"I'm going out tonight so I know I'll be tired. Plus, I have to work tomorrow anyway. I can catch up to y'all later."

"You're gonna miss all the bargains," Glory said.

"I can't imagine any bargain worth fighting those crowds," LaRone said. I could tell he had been trying to find a comfortable fit since he'd arrived. Glory hadn't exactly made it easy for him.

"Man, you must not have any women in your family. They live for those crowds and fighting over crap," Michael said.

Aunt Jeanette passed the rolls to Sweetie. "You couldn't pay me to get out there tomorrow. That's why I finished my Christmas shopping way back in September."

"I finished mine, too," Glory said. "But I still want to be in the thick of it. Frannie, you better be ready when I come to pick you up. Ain't no CP time tomorrow. Six A.M. Grandma, you need us to pick you up anything?"

"Just a little wrapping paper if you get a chance."

I gazed around the room at each one of my children and the amazing feast before us. Things hadn't been easy for me, but I certainly felt blessed. I'd done my best raising them without their fathers. At least I could say with confidence that I had been a better mother to them than my own mother had been to me.

I watched Wendell tend to his daughter and wondered what was really going on with him. A few months ago he had come to me elated and overjoyed, announcing he was going to propose marriage to a woman he'd fathered a daughter with. I could tell he was in love, maybe even for the first time. Wendell had been involved with so many women over the years, but as far as I knew, he'd never given his heart to any of them. When he turned thirty, I was afraid he would never settle down and have his own family because he never focused on any one woman in particular. Wendell was now over forty, and Naomi was the only name that I heard him mention on more than one occasion.

I wondered if my example as a woman conditioned Wendell's womanizing ways. I hated thinking like that but the truth was difficult to face. I was so happy for him the day he burst into the house showing me a ring and talking of marriage. But since then, he'd said nothing. I wanted to ask, but figured he'd tell me when he was ready.

I was certain that whatever pain Wendell felt over Naomi, Sydney made up for it. She was definitely the best thing that ever happened to him. Like any mother, I just wanted him to be happy. I also wanted to know that I'd raised a gracious man with his manhood secure and intact, even if he'd never had any real examples of that around him.

Glory was strikingly beautiful and statuesque— but also the daughter from hell. I loved her, and most of the time I even liked her, but there were times when I wanted to slap a muzzle on that mouth of hers. Times like right now. She was always jeering Frannie and provoking arguments. Unfortunately, Frannie still hadn't learned how to ignore her like the rest of us had.

Glory had a creative spirit and possessed a special gift for mixing products. She'd been conjuring up creams and conditioners for hair and skin since she was a little girl, and would sit in the bathroom for hours putting things together pretending that she was making the latest problem-solving agent for the modern woman. That wasn't her only specialty. Glory was also a man-eater. She had very little respect for men, so she used them for sex and then threw them out like trash. I wondered if that was my fault, too.

Frannie was the baby, but definitely acted like the eldest child at times. She'd been married for seven years and seemed to have every reason to be happy, but I'm not sure she really was. Michael, a great addition to our family, seemed to be a good husband to her. Busy being a wife and mother of three, she only worked one or two days a week at the shop. She seemed content in her role as housewife, but I worried about her, too. She had her sisters fooled, acting like she had it all together—but I knew better.

Sweetie, a true middle child was always overshadowed by the friction between Glory and Frannie. She was used to sitting quietly in the background while her sisters battled. I often worried about Sweetie's passiveness; she was overly trusting in relationships that never worked out.

Bryce's father, Steve, turned out to be abusive. After several interventions from Wendell, Glory, and Frannie, Steve stopped coming around. It left Bryce minus a father, but it kept Sweetie safe. Not long after, Keith showed up and tried to take over where Steve left off. Not only did he want to be Bryce's father, he wanted to be Sweetie's as well. He bossed her around and did whatever he could to humiliate her in front of others. That went on for a year until she became pregnant with his baby. During her sixth month, Keith abruptly stopped coming around.

She seemed to always be looking for love. Like me, she never had a problem getting a man. Keeping one was the issue.

Chapter 2 Sanita Parker (Sweetie)

Who you tryin' to convince, you or me?

When Robyn asked me to hang out with her, I should've gone with my first mind and stayed home. Besides the fact that I was too tired to be out in a nightclub, I had a page-turning novel on my nightstand waiting on me. A hot, steamy romance is always preferred over loud music, a smoke-filled room, and a bunch of hounds any day.

There was standing room only in the club, and I was pretty sure some fire codes were being violated. But, Robyn would've had a fit if I told her I was ready to go. Back in the day, it was nothing for us to close a club down three times a week, but I'd outgrown that. I was tired of seeing the same ol' people doing the same ol' thing. Occasionally there would be some new faces, but I just didn't care enough to be bothered.

The two-story building was dark, as well as smoky, and Robyn and I arrived too late to secure a place to sit on either level. We'd both been out on the dance floor a few times but even that hadn't changed my mood. I was turning down dances and drinks wishing we could just make an exit.

"I know that look. You're ready to go, huh?"

"Been ready," I said, just as a short, stocky brotha walked up and started talking to her. I turned my back to them and spotted a guy walking in my direction. He was a pretty boy, all dressed up in a suit, which had never been a turn on for me. Men in suits were usually anal and square. An L-7 on a pretty boy was the worst. This guy was probably the type who was all into himself.

I noticed a nervous look on his face while he glanced awkwardly around the room. *Please don't let him be on his way over here. Please don't let him be on his way... Dag.*

"Hey. How ya doin?" His voice was manlier than I expected.

"Fine." I looked him up and down and turned my head. The shoes were nice and the suit hung well. His hair was cold black, curly, and looked soft. He was a medium height with a medium build.

"What's your name?" The nervousness on his face showed up in his voice.

"What's yours?"

"I'm sorry. I'm Ric." He struggled to look comfortable.

"Oh." I gave him a fake smile.

"And yours?" he asked again.

"Sanita."

"You having a nice time, Sanita?"

"No."

"Sorry to hear that. Can I buy you a drink?"

"No, thank you."

He looked disappointed. "So, is clubbin' not your thing, or would you rather be somewhere else?"

"I'm just not in the right frame of mind tonight. I'd rather be at home with my kids."

"How many kids do you have?" He looked like he was starting to relax.

"Six." That oughta fix him.

"Oh really. I love kids. In fact, I come from a big family." He slowly nodded.

"Hmm." Like I cared.

"So, how old are your kids?"

I thought he might be trying to catch me in a lie so I attempted to count on my fingers behind my back. "Ten, eight, seven, five, and two."

He stopped nodding his head for a minute. "Umm, that's just five."

"I got a set of twins." I didn't know I could lie so easily.

"Cool. How old are the twins?" He nodded his head again.

"Two."

"You don't look like a woman with six kids."

"What does a woman with six kids look like?" I asked, with my nose turned up. I wasn't normally this mean to people and was starting to feel bad. I was ready to confess that I was lying about the six kids.

"I don't know—tired. I guess I'm just trying to say that you looking mighty fine for a mother of six. In fact…"

"Sweetie! How you doin', girl?" I turned around to find Loren Jacobs towering over me, his arms stretched wide open. Loren had been our star basketball player back in high school, and went on to play in the NBA. He'd had a crush on me since we were kids. I reached up and gave him a big hug as his lips brushed up against my cheek.

"Loren, I haven't seen you in years." He was dripping with sex appeal, but, unfortunately, I wasn't up to flirting. Loren and I had a little history. We shared one hot and steamy night of heavy petting back in school. We were really into each other, but I couldn't hang with the pressures of all the other girls that liked him, too. With the exception of that one night, we'd never been anything more than friends.

We leaned against the wall near the bar, catching up on each other's lives. His marriage, my kids, his career, and my job. It was cool seeing him, but the solitude of my home was looking better and better. Besides that, I had an early morning appointment. Loren talked on, giving me the rundown on who all he'd seen since being in town for the holiday.

"You ready?" Robyn asked, walking up.

"Girl, quit playin'," I said sarcastically.

"Hello," Robyn said to Loren.

"Loren, this is Robyn. Robyn, this is an old friend from school."

"Nice to meet you," Loren said, and then turned back to me. "You leavin' already?"

"Yeah, I've got to work in the morning. It was good seeing you though. I'm sorry I didn't get to meet your wife." I said that for Robyn's benefit.

"Maybe next time." We hugged again and Loren placed a soft kiss on my cheek. "Take care, Sweetie."

We walked to the coat check and then out of the door.

"What did ol' dude want?" she said, as the sound of our heels clicked in quick rhythm against the concrete.

"Nothing. We haven't seen each other in years—"

"Not him. The other one."

"Who? Oh, pretty boy in his church suit?" I wrapped my scarf around my head. "Girl, I don't know. And don't care."

"That's India's brother. You know my friend India at work?"

"Oh really?" I asked, looking around. "Where'd we park?"

"Over this way." She headed off to the left. "Anyway, I don't know why he was all up in your face. He's married with four kids."

"What! He didn't mention having kids or a wife." That was exactly why I couldn't stand men sometimes. They were always lying about something. I was glad I'd left him standing there looking stupid.

"Well, he's got one—a wife, I mean. He's cute though, ain't he? All of India's brothers are fine," Robyn said, as we got into the car.

"If you like that type. Which I don't." I cranked up the heat after Robyn started the engine. "Girl, hurry up and get me home."

~~~

The Friday after Thanksgiving felt more like the Saturday before Easter. Glory and Frannie were out shopping, and Mama was in the house putting up Christmas decorations. I was working alone in the shop at two o'clock in the afternoon, tired and hungry.

While both of my clients were drying, I planned to slip out of the salon and walk across the backyard to Mama's kitchen to warm up some leftovers from yesterday. But before I could, a man walked through the door of the shop holding a large bouquet. It was an assortment of wild flowers in fall colors arranged in a clear glass vase.

"Delivery for Sanita Parker."

"I'm Sanita Parker." I couldn't imagine who the flowers could've come from. "Thank you." I tried to give him a few dollars but he refused, saying the tip had been taken care of on the other end. He placed them on the front desk and walked out.

"You got a new man, Sweetie?" Brenda asked, speaking louder than she needed to because of the rushing air around her head.

"Naw. I don't know what this is." I pulled the card, which was attached to a large sunflower. I was more than a little anxious to uncover the mystery. Somebody named Ricardo, with his phone number at the bottom, saying that it had been nice meeting me last night, and he wanted to take me out. "Who in the world is Ricardo?" I mumbled to myself.

"I know I'm being nosy, girl. But who are they from?" Brenda asked. Lisa put her magazine down and waited to hear my answer.

"I don't know who this is." I tossed the card on the counter. "I'm going over to the house for a minute. I'll be right back."

I took off my apron, placed my scarf on my head, and trotted along the sidewalk across the yard.

"Sweetie, that you?" Mama yelled from the front room when I turned on the water in the sink to wash my hands.

"Yeah. I'm fixing something to eat. Where're Bryce and Anthony?"

"They're at the Y playing basketball." She entered the kitchen holding tangled Christmas lights. Her milk chocolate complexion hid, at the very least, ten to fifteen years, and her short, faintly-blond bob only added to the mystery of her age. "Sit down. I'll fix your plate. I don't want you tracking hair in my kitchen."

I sat in the corner seat at the kitchen table. That seat had belonged to me since as long as I could remember. "What have the boys been doing all day?"

"Eating. They act like they can't get enough."

Mama had turned the other side of the laundry room, where the first salon had been located, into an art studio. It looked like she was working on a new painting. I got up and wandered into the studio as we continued our conversation.

"Oh yeah, and I had them helping me hang the lights on the house," she said. "I think I wore 'em out."

"I thought Wendell was coming by to do that."

"I'm not waiting on Wendell."

I looked around to see if there were any paintings I'd missed. It had been a while since I'd snooped through her work. There was a canvas on the easel covered with a cloth. She always kept her works in progress covered until they were finished.

I pulled back the cloth. The piece was either finished, or very close to it. Abstractly done, it was a man walking through a door showing only the back of him, with a small portion of his butterscotch profile, and large Afro crowning his head. The colors were faintly shaded and shadowed with shapes like circles, squares, and rectangles—almost like a stained-glass window. That seemed to be a signature for Mama's work. On the blank edge of the canvas, written in pencil was the title "Gone." I carefully replaced the cloth and returned to the table, bringing the sadness with me that the painting offered.

"You'd better be careful getting up on that ladder," I said. "He's gonna be fussing at you."

"Oh well. He's busy, and ain't no tellin' when he would've gotten around to doing it. And anyway, I had your big ol' boys up on the ladders." She was slicing turkey and placing it on fresh bread. "Are you almost finished working?"

"I wish. I probably won't be done until about eight o'clock. You know, seems as though I put in more hours than everybody else, but I never have any money."

"Well, Frannie has a husband to pay the bills, and Glo only has herself to worry about. When you're single with kids, it's a struggle. It'll get easier, but unfortunately, not before it gets harder. Just don't keep having kids the way I did."

I looked over the plate of food Mama had put in front of me. "Oh, Ric. Ricardo must be Ric," I mumbled.

"What?" Mama asked, confused.

"Nothing."

The nerve of him to send flowers when he's married, I thought. Did I look like a woman that would screw around with a married man? I picked up Mama's phone and dialed Robyn's cell.

"Hello," she said, out of breath.

"Guess who sent me flowers? I don't even know how he found me…"

"Girl, I was gon' call you. Here's the deal. He's not married, I got him and his brother confused. I told you they all look alike. Anyway, India called me this morning, asking who I was out with last night 'cause her brother wanted to know. That's how I found out I had the wrong one."

"It doesn't matter—I ain't interested in fighting over the mirror with him. I can't stand pretty boys."

"Oh, okay."

"I'm sick of going in and out of relationships. It's time for me to spend time getting to know myself."

"I can understand that."

"But he's not married, huh?"

"Nah."

"It don't matter, he's not my type."

"You keep saying it don't matter. Who you tryin' to convince, you or me?"

"Girl, please." I picked up my sandwich and bit into it. "I'll be throwing out his number when I get back to the shop."

Chapter 3 *Wendell Parker*

I just assumed it would be that easy...

It was 2:30 in the morning and somebody was ringing my bell and knocking on the door as though there was about to be a raid on the place. I stepped into a pair of slacks and made my way down the hall, taking long strides and heavy steps.

I looked through the peephole and was not surprised to find my daughter's mother standing on the porch in a fur coat. I pulled open the door, and the cold air hit my chest.

"Naomi, what are you doing here?"

She gestured a question of 'are you gonna let me in or what?' I stood back and let her through. It wasn't the first time she'd done this in the middle of the night.

"Are you alone?" she asked softly. Although Naomi was no stranger to drama, I knew she still preferred to stay away from it when at all possible.

I disregarded her question and asked, "Why are you over here in the middle of the night? Is something wrong with Sydney?" I knew that by refusing to answer her question, she'd assume I had a woman in the bedroom.

"No. She's fine." She started wringing her hands. "Is someone here, Wendell?"

"What difference does it make? Just say what you want and leave."

Naomi removed her suede gloves, took off her coat, and sat down on the sofa. I ran a hand over my face and scratched my chin through the stubble. I could see from the determination in her eyes that it'd be hell getting rid of her.

I closed the front door. "Where're you coming from at this hour?" I knew it was none of my business, but it was obvious she wasn't coming from home. She was dressed in gray wool slacks, suede boots, and a low-cut blouse.

"Out with friends."

Of all the women I'd been with, Naomi was my one weakness. I wasn't sure if it was because she was my child's mother or if it was just her. I hated it when she caught me at weak moments like this because I needed to be on my toes to resist her. The thickness of her body and the fullness of her breasts affected me instantly. And she knew it.

"Like I said, why are you here?" I asked, as my body started to betray me.

Naomi stood and walked over to me, placing a warm palm on my chest. She moved her hand up and down my abdomen, and although I willed it to stand still, I could feel myself growing hard. She slipped her fingers inside my unbelted trousers and took a hold of me, giving a gentle squeeze.

I took Naomi by the wrist. "Naomi, don't." I looked her in the eyes so she could see that I was serious.

"Only your mouth is saying *don't*." Her hand tightened around me once more before letting go.

"If this is what you came by for, those days are over."

"Wendell, I know that you still love me." She pressed against me. I felt her breath on my face.

"What's your point?"

"Wendell…" I saw frustration rising in her face. She wanted me to make love to her, but not only that, she wanted for us to go back to the way things were before. Naomi continued, "How long are you going to punish me?"

I shook my head. Naomi was such a narcissist— she truly believed that everything I did, I did with her in mind. "I know it's hard for you to believe, Naomi, but this is not about you."

"Wendell, please."

It was funny how the tables had turned. Before we broke up, I was the one doing all of the begging and pleading.

I got her coat and opened it up for her. She reluctantly put her arms in the sleeves and turned to faced me.

"Fine, I'll go. But I *know* you still love me." She was so sure of herself. "When are you moving?"

"I'll be gone next month. But don't worry; I'll be back and forth quite a bit to see Sydney."

"I don't doubt that. I just hope you make time to see me, too."

"Look, Naomi it's late." I didn't have the strength to start up again with her.

"Okay, I'm leavin'. I just miss you so much." Her lips gently touched mine. Then she strolled to the foyer trying not to appear affected by the rejection. She opened the door and there was a tinge of misgiving on my part; I didn't expect her to comply so easily. Maybe she left because she was satisfied knowing that I was alone in the house. In fact, that may have been the real reason that she stopped by, to make sure no other woman was in her space.

"Na, I'll call you tomorrow."

I stood in the door with the cold air piercing my body, waiting on her to get into her car. When I saw the headlights backing out of the driveway, I closed the door and turned out the porch light.

Naomi, along with about twenty other women, was finding it difficult accepting my newfound lifestyle. It had been nearly five months and counting since I'd been inside a woman. Sometimes, even I didn't believe how easy it was for me to make the adjustment. One traumatic experience and I was a changed man.

The day I was to propose to Naomi was also the day we broke up. A lot of things were said that day that I know we both wish we could take back. I hated fighting with Naomi—she knew how to hit me where I lived. That night, she told me that I'd never been anything more than a good fuck to her. The fact she chose such harsh words should've told me how hurt she really was. When I walked away from her that day, I was angry with myself because I knew I had created the whole mess. Even still, Naomi words crushed me more than she'd ever really know. But, the truth hurts.

Even though we loved each other, the fact remained that sex had primarily been the basis of the relationship. When Naomi and I started seeing each other we were co-workers at Black Beauty, and she was just one of many women I was involved with. She was separated from her husband at the time, and I made it clear that I had no intention of being in a monogamous relationship with any of the women I was seeing, including her. Naomi felt totally disrespected and went back to her husband, with not so much as a hint to me or him that she was carrying my baby.

Even after Naomi was divorced, I didn't try and get back in with her because she made it clear she needed more than what I could give her. Although I knew I really cared about her, I still was not ready to commit to one woman.

Years later, when I discovered Sydney was my daughter, everything changed. I was ready to jump in headfirst and be the man I should've been trying to be all along. I was ready to be husband, father, and stepfather to Naomi's son. I wanted to build a family with Naomi. And because I was ready, I just assumed she would be ready to let go of my past also. Unfortunately, things are never quite that simple.

Because I made my mind up, I thought that would be enough for Naomi, but my old life was all around her as a constant reminder of the man I had been. Even though I never gave Naomi a reason to trust me, I just figured she would because I knew in my heart I was finished screwing around. She didn't trust me and eventually I didn't trust her—and how can two people really love each other but not trust each other make a relationship work? It could never happen.

A few months ago, I opened a Cosmetology Training Institution in Kansas City and was excited to be moving away and on with my life. It had been my dream for years and it was finally happening. The move was also allowing me to start over and take a much-needed break from women. It would be a new life—and change was so refreshing.

I only wished I could bring my sisters with me, especially Glory. Of all my sisters, she and I were the closest. Sweetie was the one we all looked out for, while Frannie tried to boss all of us around. I loved them all dearly, but Glory was my ace.

When I was about fourteen there was this one client of my mother's who'd regularly made advances towards me for some time. Even at my age I wasn't confused by the signals she was sending.

April, who was, I'm guessing thirty-ish, was a decent looking woman with large breasts and a small waistline. I was coming into my manhood at a steady pace and was pretty much horny all the time. Now, April was not my first sexual experience but it *was* my first time with someone who knew more than I did. She started out with little advances like winking and brushing up against me whenever my mother wasn't looking. That went on for a couple of months. This was back when the shop was still attached to the back of the house, and my mother, not suspecting a thing, asked me if I could walk April to her car.

I quickly agreed to do it. It was a cold autumn night so I threw on my coat, walked April to her dark blue Monte Carlo, which was approximately two doors down. I was eager to see if she was just frontin' with all of her flirting. My excitement overruled my nervousness.

We made our way down the sidewalk; all the while she was laughing, talking to me, and touching my arm. When we reached her car, she asked me to sit with her while it warmed up. We got into the car and she cranked the engine and turned on the radio. It didn't take her long to get right to the point. She asked me if I was a virgin and if I had ever been with an older woman. I told her that I wasn't a virgin and I had been waiting to get with her. Right there, she took off her pantyhose then slid her panties down from under her skirt. I leaned over and gave her a rough, awkward kiss, but she smoothed it out when she slowly kissed me back. I squeezed one of her breasts while she unzipped my pants. At some point we ended up in the back seat with me on top of her.

While I was humping away, Glory came to the car looking for me. Through the steamed windows she got a good idea of what we were doing. When I got back to the house, drained and satisfied, she was standing at the door waiting. Instead of telling on me, she was laughing, saying that she saw what that nasty lady and I were doing. She threatened to tell Joyce, but I knew she never would. It wasn't the first time she'd caught me doing something I didn't have any business doing. Glory looked out for me.

From that night on, after Joyce finished April's hair, she would pretend to leave and then double back to the basement where I would be waiting to have a quickie with her. After April got married, I would still go to her house when her husband was at work and sex her up real good. Those encounters with her marked the beginning of many years of screwing women whenever and however I could. Women became an addiction and I never could get enough.

Chapter 4 Glory Parker

...a stiff tongue and warm breath...

"Then Joyce calls me and tells me that I need to go over to Sweetie's and take her some money because her lights have been turned off. Again. Which, that ain't nothin' new, but I get over there and the lights are back on and some smooth talkin', pretty niggah is up over there wit' her. I'm assuming he's the one that got her lights turned back on. So, I ask her if she needs the money to pay him back or what. He overhears me and tells me no, that he was not looking to be repaid..."

Wendell called me up pissed because Sweetie didn't need his help. Any other time he'd be mumbling and complaining about having to bail her out of some snag she'd gotten into.

"Who is he?" I asked.

"I don't know him but I've seen him around. They call him Slick Ric. That right there ought to tell you... Looks like she's gettin' ready to get herself in some new shit. I ain't gon' be around to help her out of this one."

"Yes you will. And I will too. You just mad 'cause somebody beat you over there."

"I just don't like the fact that he probably paid the bill so he could lay up." Wendell was breathing heavily. "I'm gon' make a few phone calls and find out what dude is up to."

"Please—I'll just go over there and ask her. Call you later."

I didn't get why Wendell was so upset about Sweetie. You'd think he would be glad that somebody else already handled the situation. I realized he was just worried about her—worried about both of us, actually. Wendell wanted Sweetie and me to end up with some ol' nerdy do-gooders like Michael. Well, Michael was fine for Frannie, but Sweetie and I were attracted to the guys with a little bad-boy in them.

I wasn't sure what was really going on, but I knew how Wendell could exaggerate a situation, so I decided to check out the guy myself. Sweetie often got herself caught up with some man that ended up dogging her out and mistreating her. She was always settling for less than she deserved. Like Wendell, I didn't want to see her go through that again.

Men immediately see that I ain't for that bullshit, so that weeds the insecure ones out right off the bat. If a man were looking for a pushover, he'd find out quick that I wasn't the one. And all those brothers out there looking for a woman to take care of them, I ain't her either.

Some men assume that because I am assertive that I'm looking to be somebody's mama. But to be honest, I don't want any man in my space for too long. Doesn't matter who he is. There were only a couple of reasons to keep a man around and I wasn't in need of any of those. Having a baby was out, my house note was paid every month by me, I had an excellent mechanic to fix my Acura for the low-low, and I had no problem taking out the trash my damn self.

My attitude sounds stank I know, but I learned firsthand that men were dogs. I love Wendell dearly, but watching him screw every woman he could get his hands on was proof enough that men couldn't be trusted. And if you couldn't beat 'em, you joined 'em.

So many women had lost their minds over Wendell and some of those idiots had even turned suicidal. He forever had some drama brewing. It really was unfortunate for some of them, but I didn't have any respect for the ones that hung around begging, even when they knew there were other women. I hated to admit it, but from what I could tell, Naomi was the only one that knew how to handle Wendell. I've never cared for her as a person, but I did respect the fact that she didn't take shit from him. Not only that, she gave him a taste of his own medicine. Not by seeing other men, but by leaving him in love and strung out over her. I know for a fact that he'd never been in that position before. If he weren't my brother, and if I liked Naomi just a little bit, I would be enjoying it thoroughly.

When the phone rang again, I assumed it was Wendell calling to complain some more about Sweetie. It was a good thing I glanced at the caller I.D. first. LaRone was calling my house for the fifth time this week. He obviously had not caught the hint that I didn't want to be bothered. That's the only drawback to giving a man some sex—they want to start staking claim and making more out of a thing than what's really going on.

I was in my little makeshift laboratory next to the laundry room, working on hair cream I was developing to stop relaxed hair from breaking and shedding. I really didn't need the interruption, but as the slow tatter of the phone ringing filled the room, curiosity got the better of me.

"Hello."

"Hey! You're home. I was expecting to leave another message."

"Yes, I'm home."

"Oh-uh. How have you been?" he asked nervously. It was obvious he wasn't prepared to actually talk to me.

"I've been great. What's going on?" In other words, cut to the chase.

"Not much, not much. Umm, can I come by and talk to you?"

"I'm in the middle of working on something and then I'll be heading to Sweetie's." I had just added some lanolin and mink oil to the formula and felt like I was on the brink of something. I was learning that too many people were allergic to panthenol so I needed a substitute. The order of carrot oil had yet to arrive so I was improvising.

"It'll just take a minute."

"As I mentioned, as soon as I finish up here, I'm about to walk out. I'll be gone by the time you get here."

"I'm right outside."

"What?" I put down the vial of mink oil and glanced toward the window. "You stalking me now?"

"No. I just want to talk to you. You won't return any of my phone calls."

"Oh, so you figured you'd camp out in front of my house?"

"Nothing like that. I just really want to see you. Can I come in?"

"Umm." I peered through the blinds. Sure enough, he was leaning up against his car right outside. I replaced the lids on all of the bottles and containers. "Come on in, and make it quick."

Moments after I hung up the phone, he rang the bell. I already had my coat on, ready to go over to Sweetie's so I picked up my Coach for emphasis.

"So, you really *are* leaving," he said in a cutting tone, after I opened the door to let him in.

"I don't have to lie." He was about to piss me off.

"I'm sorry. Of course you don't." He stepped in. "I guess I just feel like you've been avoiding me. You haven't returned any of my calls." LaRone was looking extra nice in a long, cashmere, camel-colored coat, complete with fresh haircut and mustache trim. Hmm.

"I didn't feel like talking."

"Okay, well, I won't take long." He followed me to the sofa and we both took a seat. "I just want to know what happened between us."

LaRone was looking so sweet. He posed as a playboy, but he was really one of those choir boys that I couldn't take for too long, and that meant his time had run out. I felt like he was only months away from making some extravagant move like proposing, and I wasn't having that. For the most part, he handled his business in the bedroom, but I could tell he was catching feelings, so I had put an end to it.

"LaRone, I hate these kinds of conversations." I was feeling restless. "What do you want from me?"

"I just want to spend time with you. Is that asking too much?" He reached out toward me. "You didn't really give us a chance."

"I'm not looking to get into a serious relationship—I told you that in the beginning."

"Are you seeing someone else?"

"No. But I want to be free to do that if that's what I choose."

"Well, what does that have to do with us spending time together? I like being in your company and I can tell you like spending time with me, too."

"I do, but I don't want you getting all serious. I don't mind us hanging out every once in a while but you can't be gettin' all caught up and trying to see me everyday."

LaRone looked a little shocked when I said this. His expression turned to humiliation, then anger.

What was funny is that men say this same shit everyday. He would think nothing of it if the words were coming out of his mouth. But, the fact was, *I* was saying it to *him,* and he didn't like it one bit.

"I'm sorry, Babe. I don't mean to hurt you. I know that sounds harsh, but I'm doing my best to be honest."

I stood and took my coat off. I didn't want to make an enemy of LaRone and it was usually in conversations similar to this that I made somebody angry and they ended up hating me. That's why I was trying to avoid this whole scene. I'd get over it if LaRone ended up mad at me, but I would rather try and keep the peace.

I stood between his legs, taking him by the hand. "Try and understand where I'm coming from."

"I'm trying," he said, as his anger slowly subsided.

"Are you really?"

"Yeah, I am." He took my other hand and stood. "I apologize for sweatin' you," he said, in a low and raspy voice.

As LaRone regained his composure, he started to appeal to me again. I reached inside his coat and put my arms around his waist, then rested my head on his chest. Slowly, I looked up and pressed my lips to his. "I don't mean to be so difficult. It's just that I need my space. I'll give you a call later. Okay?"

"Glory, you always say that but I never hear from you."

"I just don't want you to misinterpret things."

"No misinterpreting things... I just want us to be cool again. You know?" His hand slid down the small of my back and landed on the curve that awaited there.

"Don't do this... we're not ready. I'll call you and we'll make plans for a weekend and kick it."

LaRone backed me up against the wall. I felt his body harden and knew I had let things go too far. I could hear his breathing increase, signaling he was way too anxious for the sex to be any good.

"Okay, stop."

"Come on, baby. You gotta miss me a little." He kissed my neck, and that thing was starting to work.

"I do... but..."

He slid his coat off of his shoulders while our lips were locked together. Kissing, we moved to the middle of my living area, calmly removing each other's clothes. Eventually I was left standing in my Vickie's Secrets and he was down to his designer boxer briefs. When he picked me up I assumed he was taking me back to my bed, but he carried me to the other side of the room to the settee in the corner and laid me across it.

I grabbed the remote control and turned the flame and blower on in the fireplace so we didn't catch a chill in the large room. All the while, LaRone's warm, moist breath was on my neck and traveling toward my torso. He slid the straps of my bra down and artfully began sucking on one breast and then the other. After listening to me moan and groan for a while he tugged at my lavender panties while licking the insides of my thighs.

This was so typical. He thought that he could turn me out and make me reconsider my feelings with regards to a serious relationship. But, I knew all to well that this was just a stiff tongue and warm breath up against soft and sensitive flesh. A very sweet sensation I might add, but nothing more.

One thing I couldn't stand was a man who wasn't in tune to a woman's body. Guys like that, their idea of foreplay was rubbing a woman's breasts, one at a time for about thirty seconds each and then putting on a condom. No clue whatsoever about how to detect if a woman was ready for penetration or what it took to get her in the mood.

Even worse than that was the brotha who had no clue, but *thought* he was a great lover. This guy was so busy performing and using the same moves on every woman he'd ever been with, never realizing that every woman's needs were different.

LaRone was neither of those guys, but he had an even bigger problem: he was in love with a woman who could never really love him back. And until he figured that out, he was going to be in a bad way.

After several minutes of LaRone showing me his tricks with his tongue, I was climbing the walls and not wanting him to stop. But I begged him to, anyway. I hated succumbing to an orgasm with oral sex. It seemed to be such a waste. A man's lips and tongue should only be used to get a woman ready for the real deal.

I pushed him back and demanded he drop his underwear. I needed to feel him inside me, up against my walls. He removed his drawers, and I could see he was past ready. He looked as though he was on the verge of bursting. I pulled him down to the floor and straddled him as he handed me a condom. I didn't know where it came from, but he got points for that. I tore the foil open with my teeth, caressing him and giving him a show as I placed it over his erection. Slowly, I slid down onto him. He yelled out when he felt my tightness coming down on his swelling, and it only took a couple of hoola-hoop stirs from my hips before he lost it. It was all over.

I couldn't believe it! But then again, yes I could. This is exactly what I was afraid of—him not being able to deliver.

Several minutes passed while I blankly stared at his ass lying in the middle of my floor—limp, lifeless, and totally spent. He opened his eyes and attempted a smile.

"Are you fucking kidding me?" I got up. The fury growing inside me was indescribable.

"Baby, don't be mad."

"Why didn't you just leave when I told you to?"

I slammed the bathroom door behind me. I snatched two wash cloths out of the linen closet and turned on the hot water full blast. When I returned from the bathroom, he was in the same position with his arms outstretched.

"Come here baby, let me finish you off."

I was too angry to speak.

"Come on, Glory. I'm not gon' leave you hangin'."

"Fuck you!"

"Why are you so angry?" He had the nerve to appear genuinely confused.

"Look, I left a hot towel in the bathroom for you," I said, stepping into my panties and pulling my turtleneck over my head. I could see the wheels turning in his head—he was trying to think of how to fix things.

"Come on back over here. We just getting started."

"I'm gon' need you to hurry up." I pointed a hitch hiker's thumb towards the powder room.

"I can come back later."

"The hell you can."

"What's your problem?"

"My problem is you starting a fire that you couldn't put out. I was minding my own business and doing fine before you got here. And I told you to leave—but no! You just kept fucking wit' me 'til you got me going—and then don't fuckin' deliver!" I was screaming at the top of my lungs. Even I was having a hard time believing how mad I had gotten.

"I'm sorry. You're right. I was just so anxious to be with you again, I guess."

"LaRone, I gotta go and you gotta go. Okay?" I picked my jeans up on the other side of the coffee table. "Go and get cleaned up."

"I just want things to be like it was."

I gave him that, *Now what did we just talk about?,* look.

He threw his hands up. "I know. I know..." He sat up on his elbows. "Why you gotta leave? I don't want to be the only one satisfied, that's all." He crawled over to me rubbing his cheek against my knee while massaging my thigh. The condom was barely hanging on, and I was afraid he was about to make a mess on my carpet.

My anger had subsided somewhat, but it would return if that condom slipped off. I calmed myself so that this whole scene could just be over. I knew that the longer I threw a tantrum, the longer he would be there trying to plead his case.

"Really, I was on my way to Sweetie's, and I'll probably be bringing the boys back with me to spend the night."

I think he was more disappointed than I was. He thought he was going to leave me longing and yearning for more of him; instead, he was left wondering what the hell had happened. Poor thing.

Chapter 5 Francine Thomas (Frannie)

...the birds of my heart flew awaaaay.

How did we become a family of nothing but hairstylists? I don't know, but the house we all grew up in was the same house that we all, at some time or another, came back to work in. It's been more than twenty years since Joyce built the salon at the end of the backyard and turned the one that used to be attached to the house into an art studio for her painting and pottery or anything else she tried out as a hobby.

Most of the time, it was great having the family business, along with the comfort and security of my mother and sisters, close by. But, sometimes it got to be too much being around them all day, every day—especially Glory. We all tried scheduling our clients at different times so we didn't have to see each other so much, but between birthdays and holidays, we were together most of the time anyway.

Wendell was the only one who never worked at the house professionally. All of us girls did hair alongside Joyce the minute we received our licenses. Becoming hairstylists seemed to be the natural thing for us to do, and we all ended up right there in the shop with her. Sweetie tried working at another salon for a minute but hated it. She worked like a Hebrew slave day in and day out, with clients stacked on top of each other, trying to make ends meet. She was back at Joyce's shop in less than a month.

Glory, well, Glory was the rebel. She was constantly pursuing other careers, and had dabbled in everything from real estate, to managing a chain of clothing stores, to peddling her own skin and hair care products. But she always ended up back at the shop, too.

For me, I did hair to make my own money, so I didn't have to go to Michael for any or explain what I'd spent mine on. And whenever I wanted to take time off, I did. That was definitely one of the advantages to being married and working in this profession. I didn't have to worry with regard to losing my job. I may lose a couple of clients, but for me that wasn't really a big deal since I didn't have to be concerned about making enough money to live off of. After all, a client dropping off here and there was the nature of this business anyway.

Michael wanted me home with the kids, but he also enjoyed the extra money I brought in. Once I saved practically every dime I made for six months, working long hours, and paid for a five-day trip to Disney World for him, the kids, and me. After I paid for the trip, there was almost five thousand dollars left over for spending. We had the best time eating and spending money like crazy. I love being able to do those kinds of things for my family. And I love taking care of them too—most days anyway. But taking care of everyone's needs can be stressful at times, which I don't think anyone truly understands.

My mother and sisters think life is easier for me because I'm married. And since none of them have ever been married, they think I have it made. They don't realize the pressure I'm under trying to keep up the ideal family life just so they aren't disappointed. The stress sometimes is too much, so I use food to help deal with it all.

I certainly wasn't built like *Barbie* when Michael and I met, but I'm sure this wasn't what he expected either. He just doesn't have the heart to complain about my weight. Instead, he drops hints by buying us family memberships to health clubs and gyms. He's physically fit and can't understand why I don't get it together.

The more concern I have about getting on the scale, the more I want to eat. Sometimes I find myself sneaking off to get food, three, maybe four times a day, in addition to eating at regular mealtimes.

I know for some overweight people, food controls them just as crack does a crack addict. You'd think because I know this, it would be easy for me to give up the binges. But I can't let them go. It is so bad, I often order extra drinks at fast food restaurants so it won't appear that all of the food I order is for me. It is a habit that both disgusts and embarrasses me.

Last week, I stopped to get doughnuts. I went with the intention of getting half a dozen to snack on throughout the day, but when I got to the drive-thru speaker, I decided to get a whole dozen and take some home for my family. It had been a particularly stressful week, so I took a moment in the parking lot of Krispy Kreme to eat a couple while they were still hot. I began focusing on all the things that needed to be done that day: the teacher appreciation brunch I volunteered to organize for Mikie's class, the cake I needed to bake and deliver for a bereaved family at church, getting Ericka to her doctor's appointment on time, and getting home to meet the school bus and to start dinner. Before I knew it, there were three doughnuts left. I didn't even remember eating over half the box.

I'd tried every diet that had ever been invented, but couldn't give up food. I'd failed them all.

This probably sounds like an excuse, but being in a family of perfectly fit women made things that much more difficult for me. Besides the fact that on most days Joyce looked younger than me, she'd never worn larger than a size eight.

I'd never been thin like the rest of them. Glory, at five-eleven, was all legs and hair. Sweetie was average height for a woman, and her body was firm, perfect, and identical to Joyce's. I was the one that didn't fit in. Glory was the only one that ever made reference to my weight while we were growing up, but I was determined not to let her know how much it bothered me. Unfortunately, she didn't have any physical flaws that I could tease her about, so I retaliated by calling her an evil heifer and hateful bitch.

Aside from that, we all got along well growing up, and had a lot of fun as children. We were united as a family. As most siblings, we would fight each other but dared anyone else to bother any one of us. Glory beat up many kids that picked on Sweetie and me, and

Wendell did a lot of fighting where Glory was concerned. We had each other's backs.

We did the average things that children did growing up. We held our own dance contests and talent shows. We'd also play school and church. Joyce wasn't a regular Sunday goer, but she made sure we attended all services. The church bus picked us up for Sunday school and Vacation Bible School when she was too tired or busy to take us. When we joined the choir, she always made sure we got there if she was working at the shop. Since we spent so much time there, it was one of the things we most enjoyed imitating.

When we played church, Wendell pretended to be the preacher and Glory was always the lead singer in the choir. They rarely ever let Sweetie and me act out what we wanted. Sweetie never complained, but I used to throw a fit and threaten to tell on them. Wendell would insist that girls couldn't be preachers. Glory said that I couldn't sing well enough to lead a song, so they made me play the imaginary piano. Sweetie was what we called the Holy Ghost lady—she would run around the room screaming and shouting until she fell out on the floor.

Wendell would do his best imitation of Reverend Sims, our Pastor, and we would end each service with the passing of an old Frisbee as our collection plate, which also doubled as the tambourine. Our closing song was "At The Cross." We made up most of the words because we couldn't remember them. We sang it wrong for so long that as an adult, I still struggle to sing the correct words. It almost comes out, 'At the cross, at the cross, where I first found a knife and the birds of my heart flew awaaaay.' We all laugh thinking of it now, and I bet they're all fighting back the same urges when they hear certain songs we used to sing down in the basement as kids.

It was strange now because Joyce, who wasn't the most religious woman, was now in church every time we turned around. All of us go regularly except Wendell. He won't set foot in a church. Once he was out on his own, he never went to church again that I knew of. And he wouldn't really speak on it either. I wasn't sure what happened, but I knew that when we were kids, Wendell used to be close to Rev. Sims and his wife. He used to go over to their house all the time and worked at the church. But suddenly, all of that came to an end. He just stopped going. Soon after, so did we.

There was a rumor that Joyce was messing around with Rev. Sims way back when. I often wondered if that was why Wendell stopped working at the church. Around that time, Wendell also stopped wanting to play church. He and Glory were both growing up and acting as though they didn't have much time for games anymore.

On fall and winter nights when we weren't allowed to stay out late, we would go to the basement and pretend to be a singing group, practicing our singing and dance moves all night long. We would go through Joyce's records, listening to The O'Jays, Sly and the Family Stone and Gladys Knight and the Pips. She didn't really mind us playing the 45's, but was touchy with regard to her albums. One of our favorites was The Stylistics' "Have You Seen Her." We practiced that one over and over.

Wendell did the speaking part of the song, and Glory of course did the lead singing. Sweetie and I were left to do back-up, which we didn't mind so much because that meant we got to do all of the latest dance moves.

Coming in with a deep voice, Wendell would start out, "One month ago today, I was happy as a lark..." while our backs were turned to the imaginary audience. Then we would spin around and sing, "Oh, I see her face everywhere I go, on the streets, and even at the picture show. Have you seen her? Tell me, have you seen her?" popping our fingers and moving from side to side.

That was one of our favorite songs to perform because everyone was happy with their part. Then one day I asked if I could do Glory's part, just once. I used to love the way she would sing the part that went *'Why, oh why did she have to leave and go away?'* I just wanted to sing it one time.

Glory was standing by the record player ready to put the LP on the turntable when I started throwing a fit. I kept asking for them to let me do it just that once. When she kept saying no, I snatched the record out of her hands. She snatched it back. Just as Wendell was coming over to take the record away from both of us, I grabbed at it one last time and it went flying across the room, sliding under the divan. Side A, which had our song on it, was scratched so badly that we couldn't listen to it. Joyce was so mad at us. After tagging each of us a couple of times with a belt, she dared us to touch her record player for a month, which pretty much ended our careers as the next big singing group.

As adults, I'm the only one who still sings in public, as a member of the adult choir at Dellrose United Methodist. Glory and Sweetie both had better voices than I did, but I was the only one using what God blessed me with. Everybody else was busy—busy making poor decisions and messing up their lives.

Chapter 6 *Joyce*

...consequences to suffer...

"Glo got away with not helping with Thanksgiving, but that's not happening for Christmas."

"We handled everything okay, Frannie."

"Well, I think we should make her do the whole Christmas breakfast by herself."

I had been listening to Frannie rant about Glory for the past twenty minutes. I realized years ago when they were just girls that Glory and Frannie would forever be at odds, involved in a life-long argument.

It was promising to be a hot summer's day, and I had the girls up at seven o'clock that morning helping me in the beauty shop attached to the back of the house. I would shampoo and press their hair in between my appointments while they worked. They would walk around all day with fat, nappy twist balls all over their heads, sweeping up hair, and straightening magazines while waiting on me to get around to pressing their hair. When I knew I would be really busy, I would do

Glory's hair the night before because I depended on her the most for help, and also because Glory grew enough hair for ten people, and it would take a lot longer to get through her tresses.

Frannie, who was eight years old at the time, was sitting under the hair dryer. She asked Glory, who was about twelve and already a head taller than me, to walk to the store for her. Frannie always kept money stashed somewhere so she gave Glory twenty-five cents to walk down eleventh street, north on Grove, and over to IGA, to buy her a bag of Guy's barbeque potato chips. Glory walked out with Frannie's quarter and made the trip that all of them had made so many times before. Sweetie sat in the hydraulic chair while I combed through her big bush of wet tangles and Frannie sat across the room with her chubby legs dangling just short of the floor, anxiously awaiting Glory to return with her bag of chips.

A little while later, Glory walked back through the screen door, letting it slam even though I'd often threatened their lives for that very thing. With a quick glance of apology towards me, Glory went straight to sweeping and putting away hair rollers.

"Glo, where's my chips?" Frannie asked, mouth watering for a snack. Glory ignored Frannie. I pretended to ignore them both, engrossed in a conversation with one of my Saturday regulars, who was underneath the hair dryer next to Frannie.

Sweetie looked at Glory, then back at Frannie as if she were a spectator at Wimbledon. She was waiting on Glory to hand over the bag of chips probably so she could beg Frannie for one.

After calling Glory's name a few times Frannie started huffing and puffing. "Glo! Where's my chips?" she yelled across the room.

Glory turned and looked at Frannie, just as everyone else did in the small and close space. Through the mirrors, Sweetie watched me as I looked at Frannie as if she'd lost her mind.

"Oh—I ate 'em," Glory finally answered.

Tears welled up in Frannie's eyes. "You ate my chips?"

"*Yeah,*" Glory added, as if she wanted to know what Frannie was going to do about it.

Frannie was mad. "Why'd you eat my potato chips?"

"Cuz I wanted to." Glory sucked her teeth and continued replacing rollers on the roller stand.

Frannie shot out from beneath the dryer hood and dove in with both fists swinging. Because Glory was long and lanky, she was able to dodge Frannie. Instantly, a rainbow of red, yellow, blue, and green cylinders floated and spiraled into the air, then scattered all over the floor. Glory shoved Frannie and her plump behind hit the linoleum and slid.

After letting out a myriad of cuss words, I broke it up and whipped them both, and then made them clean up the mess. Nothing more was ever said with regard to the quarter or the bag of chips.

That day was just one of many over the years of name-calling, boyfriend-stealing, hair-pulling, biting, and scratching. You would think that the premise for these arguments would have evolved into more important issues, but I'm afraid not.

I'd always wanted my children to be close as siblings—unlike the relationship I had growing up with my own immediate family. I had a sister and two brothers. I was the second born and my father's only reason for coming home every day. I knew this because he told me so. I was the rebellious one, and Daddy encouraged it, because I reminded him of himself when he was young. He told me that, too.

Daddy died when I was thirteen, leaving my mother to raise four children alone. She tried her hardest to keep up appearances and a certain way of life, only to discover it was more difficult than she imagined. She was always struggling to maintain the status she fooled herself into believing she possessed. Two years later, when she discovered I was pregnant at fifteen, it was as if the end of the world had come upon the whole family.

The only thing worse than having my family shun me was having Nathan leave me to suffer the consequences alone. Nathan was my first love, and I was crushed when he left me to fend for myself. It wasn't until I saw my beautiful baby boy that I felt like all of the whispering, looks of disappointment, and ridicule was worth it. I wanted my son to grow and become a man like my father so I gave him my father's name: Wendell. I showered him with the same affection and favor my father showered me with.

Before I could be forgiven by my family, at the age of seventeen I had to relive the nightmare. And that would be the pace I set for myself four times. All of my children fathered by different men with the exception of Wendell and Glory; at least, that is what everyone assumes, even Nathan.

I never really knew for sure which of the two boys I was intimate with was Glory's father, and I was not about to say anything different. Having two children out of wedlock had brought enough wrath upon me. I couldn't let on that I was unsure which of the two boys I was intimate with was Glory's father.

It was my younger sister Jeanette's disappointment that hurt me the most. We had always been close, but when I ended up pregnant, she called me a whore for getting pregnant, which was, to her, different than just having sex. Jeanette was valedictorian of her class and went on to Howard University. By the time Jeanette graduated with her bachelor's degree in elementary education, she was engaged to an engineer. They were married in a huge church wedding and Jeanette invited all of her college friends to be bridesmaids.

I was pregnant with Sweetie at the time, and Jeanette didn't think it would look right having her unmarried pregnant sister standing up in front of God as her witness. So, I stood behind the podium for the guest book, feeling unworthy. Not that I would've been comfortable standing down front with a big belly, but it would've been nice for her to want me there.

Although they tried for years, Jeanette and her husband were unsuccessful at having children. Because we both had what the other wanted, we wasted a lot of time envying each other. Several years after burying her husband, she moved back to town.

We all took turns disappointing my mother, it seems. My older brother James was on his way to college—pre-med. He had scholarships awaiting him and important people in the community mentoring and supporting him. Then one Friday night during his senior year in high school, he was with some friends when they stopped at a liquor store to buy a bottle of Southern Comfort to pass around. While James waited in the car with the driver, one thing led to another and the storeowner was robbed at gunpoint. They were all sentenced to ten years in Leavenworth.

For James, the prison door has been a revolving one ever since. Before he got in trouble, he had shunned me like the rest of the family had. But once his freedom was taken away, he realized I was the only one he could depend on to write and visit him on a regular basis.

Joseph, the baby in the family, never outwardly held animosity toward me. But he never came to my defense either. He exerted most of his energy worrying about how the family would accept his attraction to men. He must have concluded that him being a homosexual would be a fate worse than mine, because he chose to fade into the background and stay in the closet.

It took some time before my mother learned to appreciate her grandchildren. They were practically teenagers before she resigned herself to the fact that they were the only ones she would be blessed with. Eventually she embraced them, as did Jeanette, James, and Joseph. At one point, I thought they would be ashamed of me forever, but gradually, and eventually, all was forgiven. The children never seemed to know any different.

I'd always felt a mother's joy where Wendell and the girls were concerned, and was satisfied that I was the one to carry on my father's name, further proof that

Wendell Parker once walked this earth. If he could look down now, I believe he would be pleased. He never would have turned his back on me; and how he would have loved his grandchildren, just as I do.

I'm not ashamed of the life I've lived, but I'm not really proud of it either. I've had a few husbands over the years; none of them were mine, but I'd had them. I took love any way I could get it. And now I wonder if the punishment for my many affairs would be never having someone of my own, someone that would love only me. Like anyone else, all I ever wanted was to be cared for and have companionship.

Thankfully, being married isn't as important to me now as it had been in the past. Back when appearances meant more to me, I was desperate for someone. But I'd grown up—a lot. There had been consequences to suffer for the choices I'd made and none of them were worth it. With one exception— Carlos.

If fate allowed me the chance to relive the time with Carlos, I would do everything the same. After all these years, thinking of him still makes me feel warm inside and happy, sad, loved, and lonely all at the same time. Happy because I knew him, sad because he's gone. Loved because of the way he loved me, and lonely... because of the way he loved me. There has never been another like him. Living in the past can be a pathetic and depressing enigma, but not when it comes to my memories of Carlos. It was the memories of him that kept me from settling for a lesser man.

I first laid eyes on Dr. Carlos Espinoza at the County Hospital. Glory, less than a year old at the time, continuously feverish and lethargic, had been admitted into the hospital for severe dehydration. However, her illness continued to get worse until the day the most beautiful black man I'd ever seen walked into the hospital room. At that time, doctors who were men and women of color were rare, and Dr. Espinoza was a pediatrician with a soothing hand and a gentle spirit. It was obvious that he loved caring for children.

Carlos read Glory's chart and thoroughly examined her. When he called me into his office and asked me if I was alone, I thought he was going to tell me that my baby wasn't going to make it. I told him I was there by myself and began crying. I considered calling Mama for a moment, but changed my mind because we were still on shaky ground.

Carlos took hold of my hand and told me that Glory had been misdiagnosed. She had rheumatic fever. He explained that she would more than likely be fine, but would need to stay in the hospital a week.

During that time, Carlos tended to Glory night and day, making sure the nurses were following his strict instructions for her care. Glory's already sparse hair had fallen out from the high fever, and he would rub her little head, promising in a soft whisper that one day she would have long beautiful hair. When I saw him giving his other patients the same love and attention, I knew just what kind of man he was. Under his excellent care, Glory was well in no time.

Our relationship didn't begin right away. It was some time after Glory was released from the hospital that Carlos began calling me at home to check on her. When he made a house call to examine her, a romance was instantly sparked.

Carlos was originally from the east coast, but he lived in Hutchinson and commuted home on the weekends. I knew he was married, even though he didn't tell me in the beginning. I felt guilty once the relationship began to develop and we fell in love, but it didn't stop me from wanting to be with him.

It was six months into our relationship when he finally spoke of his wife and two small boys. He didn't say much about them, and I didn't ask. Whenever he was with Wendell, Glory, and me, he treated us as though we were his family. He loved us like we were his family. In fact, once we moved in together, he spent more time with us than he did with his first family. It was the happiest time of my life, and I believe in my heart it was the happiest of his, too.

Carlos was a young doctor with a lot of responsibility and stressful work. I was even younger and just happy to be loved by such a magnificent man. A year passed and we built a life together, as much as was possible under the circumstances. He never spoke directly of leaving his wife, but would say things like, "One day soon, Wendell and Glory will be able to call me Daddy." I believed he loved them as much as he loved his own children.

The day I suspected I was pregnant, I was apprehensive about telling him. He never expressed any disappointment where our relationship was concerned, and I was afraid this might be the one time that he did. It was going on midnight when he came home, exhausted from the hospital. I wanted to put off telling him until he was rested, but also knew he loved me and would want to know. Once he slid into bed, he put his arms around me and kissed my shoulder. He could barely keep his eyes open. I turned over and told him I needed to tell him something that couldn't wait. He sat up in bed and did his best to give me his full attention.

After the words left my mouth, Carlos was fully alert. He stared at me for a few moments, and then a tear welled up in the corner of his eye. He hugged me and told me he loved me. Then he said, and I remember his exact words, "Joyce, you deserve better than what I've been giving you. I promise you, I'll fix this." It was supposed to be the beginning of our life together.

In the beginning, he was going to Hutchinson every Friday and back again on Monday. Eventually he made those trips less and less, but not because I asked him to. He never got any pressure from me. I wanted to be his refuge and believed I was just that.

Everything changed on a cold Thursday in January, nineteen degrees to be exact, and much less than that with the wind chill factored in. I was eight months pregnant and an ice storm was predicted to pass through overnight. Earlier that evening, something happened I never saw coming: Carlos' wife called our home.

When she announced that she was Josephine Espinoza, I didn't have to guess who she was. I sat there stunned as she informed me that she knew about the baby coming. She asked me question after question that I refused to answer. I told her to speak to Carlos.

Josephine never once raised her voice, and I could tell she was trying to hide her weeping. Her voice was unsteady as she asked me if I loved Carlos. I held the phone in silence; she understood. As she sniffed and struggled to speak, I understood, too. We were two women desperately in love with the same man. I never thought that Carlos didn't love Josephine; I never tried to fool myself about that. But, I *knew* he loved me. He was just committed to her.

I promised her I would ask Carlos to call when he came "home." She was understandably upset and frustrated. According to her, several weeks had passed since she'd seen him, and it had been a week since she'd heard from him. I put myself in her shoes and the truth of the whole thing left me feeling sick.

For the first time, reality set in. Carlos' wife was real to me and so was the predicament I was in— carrying a married man's baby. I waited up for him that night in the front room of our cozy two-bedroom apartment, looking around at our love nest. We had built what I thought was a real life. We even had a routine. Every morning I sent him off to the hospital after a hot breakfast, often packing him a lunch of leftovers from a dinner I had prepared the night before that he'd more than likely missed. Consistently around 3:00 A.M., Glory would wake up calling for him and he'd go to her, rocking her back to sleep.

When Carlos walked in, he knew immediately something was wrong. He thought I was having contractions until I told him that his wife was expecting a call from him. He never asked me about our conversation; he just apologized, sat next to me, and picked up the telephone. I moved to leave the room, but he stopped me, saying that he'd been putting things off for too long.

I sat there listening to his side of the conversation, trying to fill in the blanks of what was being said on the other end. I could hear her muffled voice, but couldn't discern any of her words. His responses were, "Yes, I love her," "Over a year," and "Eight months," intermingled with some yes's and no's.

It seemed as though her questions would never end. The guilt was torture for me, so I could only imagine how he felt. Carlos finally agreed to go home so that they could talk things out.

After he hung up the phone, I began begging him not to go. I pleaded with him to wait until the morning. There was a foreboding coming over me, and I knew if he left, things would never be the same. What if he saw her and changed his mind about us? He promised he would be back the next day, and when he came back, he would be staying for good. He said to trust him; he was going to work it all out. He apologized for putting me through so much and told me he owed Josephine an explanation and an apology in person. He rubbed my swollen belly and kissed my pouting lips. His last words were, "Trust me. I love you and I promise I'll be right back."

Carlos never came back, and he never made it to Hutchinson either. Somewhere along the way, the ice which was predicted began to fall. I never found out the details of the accident. I never got a phone call that a wife would get. I couldn't publicly mourn the loss of the man that loved me, the father of my unborn baby. I couldn't put him to rest. I received no condolences or sympathy cards. In the twinkling of an eye, I was alone again.

I was devastated to say the least, and the agony of Carlos's death threw me into premature labor. In a total of three hours my love child was born. Sanita Espinoza Parker. Carlos' only daughter had been brought into the world fatherless—just as her brother and sister before her.

Chapter 7 *Sweetie*

Love clearly was on the way.

This must be how Janie felt when Tea Cake told her she held the keys to the kingdom. I wasn't sure if I was in desperate need of attention or if Ric was really my Prince Charming, but he was starting to grow on me. I hadn't completely let my guard down, but I had definitely let him get his foot in the door. I was trying not to rush things, but he possessed a passion I'd been missing in every other relationship that I'd had, which made me want to hurry things along.

I never called him after he sent the flowers, but he persisted, and one night caught me in a weak moment. The boys were spending the night at Glory's, and I was alone with nothing to do. I figured a nice meal I didn't have to pay for was enough for me at the time.

When Ric arrived, I didn't know what to think. There he was, standing at my door, holding a small, white teddy bear with a purple bow, looking nervous again. "Hi, Sanita," he said, handing me the token of affection.

I tried to remember if any of my prior dates or boyfriends ever stood at my front door with a gift in hand when they came to pick me up. I couldn't think of one. It was a small gesture, but because it was a first, it turned monumental.

"Aw." I stepped back to let him in. I took the bear and pressed it up against my face, unable to hold back a smile.

"You look really nice," Ric said, looking me up and down. "I hope this doesn't sound corny, but I had forgotten how pretty you are."

"Thanks," I said, blushing. I sat the teddy bear on the banister and let him help me with my coat. We walked down the sidewalk and up to a white Hummer. As he opened the door for me, I began to feel uncomfortable, wondering exactly what kind of man Ric was. How was he able to afford a ride like this?

I could pretend that a thousand things weren't running through my mind, but I had been through too much with men. I wasn't sure I was even feeling him anyway, so it was better for me to get a clear understanding of who he was up front.

"I'm really glad you decided to hang out wit' me tonight," he said, getting in on the driver's side. "Since you didn't return my calls, I was startin' to think you weren't interested."

Little did he know, I *wasn't* interested in him. I happened to get off of work early and just wanted to get out of the house.

Ric made nervous chatter while he searched for the right CD to put in. I debated over whether or not to voice my suspicions concerning him. It was of little consequence to me, so in the middle of him asking what type of food I had a taste for, I just blurted it out.

"What kind of work do you do?" I could feel the lines in my forehead and the frown on my face but I doubted if he could see any of that in the dark. I know he heard it in my voice, though.

"Umm. Well, actually I'm in between. I begin training for a new job on Monday."

"Doing what?"

"Pharmaceutical sales."

"What did you do before?" I looked around at the plush interior of the Hummer. I couldn't think of any legitimate profession that paid well enough for him to afford such an expensive automobile other than sports or entertainment, and I was fairly certain he wasn't involved in either.

Ric cleared his throat and pressed a button to open the sunroof. I couldn't figure out why he wanted it open when it was so cold out—except to show off. As if reading my thoughts, he turned up the heat.

"Sanita, I'm not gon' lie. I did my thang out on the streets for a while. But I'm through with all that now."

I knew it. In his Polo sweater and brown, leather Cole Haans, he looked like a Buppy who had just graduated from college. But underneath it all, I sensed he was up to no good. That was okay, though. It was just dinner. I hadn't expected much anyway.

"So, basically you're just legalizing your profession with your new job." I was sure he heard my sour tone draped all around that comment.

"I hope you don't let that keep you from getting to know me," he said. He sounded sad.

"How long has it been since you've stopped?"

"Recently. But, I'm serious. I'm done with it."

"Well, I have some strong opinions about drug dealers that I'm sure you won't like."

He frowned. "My new job is completely legit. Look, I'm not proud of my past, but there's more to me than that. I won't make excuses, but that was what I thought I had to do at the time. It was easy to get into and it was even easier to make plenty of money. But, after a while it wasn't so easy anymore, and the money wasn't worth the risks I was facing. So, I got out before I was forced out for other reasons."

Ric seemed to be sincere, but that didn't mean I had to involve myself in his drama. I was ready to get this dinner over and done with and go back to my quiet life.

"Well, Ric, I appreciate your honesty. We can be friends, but I gotta be honest as well—I don't know if I can respect a man that has made his living doing that."

"Sanita, I don't want anything from you. Let's just have dinner and a nice time tonight. Okay?"

I softened. "You know, I'm sorry. I don't mean to be so judgmental. I just have strong feelings about that. That's all."

"You don't have to apologize. I respect the way you feel."

There was a sweetness to Ric. I expected him to have an attitude or be defensive, but instead, he continued to extend kindness and respect towards me. He seemed to be enamored with me in a way that was unexpected. Careful not to offend and anxious to impress me, he was still a little nervous; but at every chance, he continued to show me that I was a lady. And I could tell that it wasn't an act. I got the feeling he was determined to show me how a man was supposed to tend to a woman. And after some of the fools I'd dealt with, I *needed* somebody to show me.

We ended up at a five-star restaurant. Maybe he thought that's what I expected, when I would've been satisfied with the local bar and grill. I found Ric to be intelligent and humorous as he showed me a softer side of himself.

Ric kept me entertained with stories of growing up with ten brothers and sisters. We got the children thing straightened out on both sides. He teased me about the six kids I said were running around my house.

All and all, it was a nice evening, but I was still determined to not let myself be interested in a person that ever thought it was okay to distribute poison in the community. I just wasn't going to do it.

Well... what I thought was going to be a one time date, quickly turned into something more. The next day, I had just returned home to find my electricity shut off when Ric showed up unannounced. He apologized for not calling first, and then held out my scarf, which I had left in his car the night before. Instinctively, I invited him in.

As we stood in the entryway making small talk, he finally clued in that the room was cold. Then he noticed there were no lights, music, or television on.

"Sanita, everything okay?"

"I just forgot to pay the bill," I said. "I'm gonna handle it."

"Can I help you out?"

"I'm on my way to take care of it right now." I dropped my head. "This is so embarrassing."

"Don't be… Let me help you."

"Thanks for the offer, but I really do have it under control."

"Now, what kind of man would I be to walk out of here leaving you like this?" He pulled out his cell phone and made a call.

"Yo, man. What's up? …What area you working right now? Yeah… Right now, if you can." I listened to him rattle off my address as if it was his own, and then he disconnected the call.

"Where are your kids?"

"They're at my mother's."

"It's gonna be about twenty minutes or so. Do you want to go and sit in my car?"

"No. I'm fine," I said through chattering teeth and breath that hung stationary in the air.

"Well, at least put on a coat." He began blowing warm breath into his hands and rubbing them together.

I grabbed my coat and took a seat on the bottom step of the staircase. Ric joined me and began talking, obviously trying to get my mind off my apparent problems. Fifteen or twenty minutes later I heard the hum of my refrigerator and the heat kick on.

"I'll be right back." Ric walked out the door and around to the side of the house. I peeked out the dining room window and saw him talking to a young white guy who was refusing to take his money. I moved away from the window and went to the kitchen to check the contents of the refrigerator. When Ric walked back in the house I was pouring out the milk as a precaution.

"How much do I owe you?" I asked.

"Don't worry about it."

"Who was that?"

"Someone who owed me a favor."

"One of your customers?" The uncomfortable feeling was back. I suddenly regretted letting him help me.

"No, not at all. Don't be so suspicious. It's taken care of. You don't owe me anything. Even if I never hear from you again, okay?" He smiled. "Although, I hope that's not the case."

"Let me pay you whatever was owed on the bill," I insisted.

"Like I said, he owed me a favor. You're taken care of."

I raised an eyebrow. "Is this legal?"

"Trust me; he'll take care of it. Again, don't be so suspicious." I eyed him as he spoke. "It's gonna be fine."

"I guess I should be thanking you, but I can't help but ask questions."

"It's all right." He looked at his watch. "Well, I need to get going. Unless you need something else."

Initially I feared Ric might feel as though I owed him something, but he never brought it up again. He was actually very careful not to force his way into my life, even though I could tell he was anxious to connect with me. He knew that I was alone raising the boys, and probably felt compelled to try and take care of me. I got that a lot from the men I dated. The only difference was that the others wanted to control me, while Ric didn't. He made sure I had what I needed, and never asked for anything in return. I loved it.

Ric spoiled me rotten. He would call me throughout the day and have lunch delivered to me at the shop. He was always taking my car to get detailed and returning it with a full tank of gas. He did whatever he could to try and make life easier for me.

The week Ric was supposed to begin his on-the-job training, he found out he didn't make security clearance. Apparently something he thought had been expunged from his record was still showing up. He didn't go into a lot of detail, but I could tell he was really down. He was trying so hard to make a new life for himself by leaving the streets, and I wanted to comfort him. After all, he had been so sweet to me.

Needless to say, the setback eventually made Ric lose his drive. At first, he acted as though he was going to make another go at it. He had earned a degree and knew he could still get work, or so he thought. He never mentioned what other fields he tried to enter, but I think he made some efforts and was still being turned away based on his past.

Ric's means of escape from his situation was showering me with gifts. It was a little overwhelming at first, but it didn't take me long to become spoiled by the attention. Money for groceries, getting my car repaired, a new outfit when he was taking me somewhere special. I'd never been treated so well.

Several months passed before Ric and I crossed the line into intimacy. He was careful not to come on too strong, waiting for me to give him the green light. After many nights of passionate necking, heavy petting, and plenty of blue-ball-ending dates, I finally did. Ric took me away on a four-day excursion to Rocky Mountain National Park in Boulder, Colorado. The high altitude and romance seeping from the snow-covered mountains was all it took.

After several attempts to convince me that I could afford to take off of work, of course with his help, I got the boys situated at Glo's and joined him in the mountains to ski. Or not ski. And not ski was pretty much how it turned out for me. It was my first time, and he was by no means an expert but he knew how to handle the snow better than I did. He was a patient teacher, but we spent the majority of our time in the condominium he'd rented sitting in front of a large picture window watching the snow fall.

"Now, tell me you're not glad to get away." Ric asked me. We'd been out for several hours and were happy to return to the warmth of the ski lodge.

"Of course, I'm glad. I just didn't think that it was possible for me to rearrange my clients without a lot of backlash, that's all. I don't ever mind getting away."

"Well, I'm glad that you're glad." We sat cuddled together in what had become our favorite spot. Ric pulled me close and kissed me with such passion and heartfelt emotion. He'd moan as he ended his kisses and then break away as if my kisses were some succulent dessert he'd been craving. Then he'd slowly open his eyes as though he needed the moment to linger on in sweet remembrance.

After Ric started a fire, he made two Bailey's and coffee for us in the small kitchenette, and we sipped and chatted.

"I can't remember a time when I was this content. There is a peacefulness about you that I don't ever want to be without." His admission caught me off guard. I knew Ric enjoyed my company but him being so open was foreign to me. "Sanita, you make me want to be a better man."

Not knowing what to say, I gently touched his face and hoped the gesture communicated my sentiments.

Once dinner had been delivered along with a bottle of wine, a new us had been born and a romantic void I didn't even know existed was filled.

As far as I could remember, no one had ever tried to please me in bed the way Ric did. He was anxious to bring me pleasure. I'd never had a lover so in to me, and I relished it.

"Are you comfortable?" Ric asked me, right before he proceeded to remove my bra and panties.

"Very," I said, whispering in his ear.

"Good." He continued by kissing my neck. I loved Ric's gentleness and his caring nature. I didn't want to believe that I had fallen in love with Ric yet, but I knew it was coming. Love clearly was on the way.

"I want you to be comfortable."

"Ric, I'm fine," I moaned in response to his touch.

"I just want you to feel good," he said, looking me in the eyes. And I did. "I'll go only as far as you want me to. Okay?"

And I believed him but I had no intention on asking him to stop.

After making love, we laid together in each other's arms. Ric fell into a deep sleep with his arms wrapped around me. His slumber was so absorbed as if he hadn't slept that peacefully in a long time. I remained perfectly still and fell asleep with him and our breathing became rhythmically in sync.

After a couple of hours, I awakened and changed positions breaking away from Ric.

"Are you okay?" Ric asked, startled and half awake when I moved from him. His attentiveness was very flattering at the time and of course I didn't see the beginning of something else. "Do you need anything?"

"I'm fine—just going to the bathroom."

Once I returned to the bed Ric and I enjoyed each other's bodies over and over again until the sun came up. A new addiction was beginning to replace an old one, but I had no way of knowing that then. I was too enthralled with the new heights of pleasure that my body and soul was experiencing. A man behaving as though his very sustenance of life depended on whether or not I was comfortable or taken care of was something that I never imagined could happen. And after being neglected for so long I soaked it up like a sponge. The idea of it being so unhealthy went unnoticed by me but when two damaged people came together the only thing that could follow was more destruction.

After we returned from Boulder we were officially a couple. Ric was my man and I was his woman. But as we began the process of integrating into each other's lives, the newness slowly faded.

Chapter 8 *Wendell*

I closed the door behind me... and took a deep breath.

"Mr. Parker? What happens when we get out on the floor and we have to do a service we don't wanna do?" TaLisa asked, standing up in front of the classroom facing me wearing a long, turquoise smock, khaki pants, and Nike tennis shoes. She was a twenty-year-old, eager to get to the demonstration part of her education.

Careful to mask my excitement, I calmly addressed the first group of students to successfully complete enrollment. "Well, first of all," I started, "it'll be a while before you're faced with that. But, everyone will have to do whatever service is on the ticket. This is how you get your experience. When you get out there in the world, you will be able, on some occasions, to pick and choose the work you want to do. But, as long as you are a student, you will be expected to do it all. That's the only way you'll be fully educated and prepared to take your State exams.

"Now is the time to get all of the experience that's available to you. During the course of this program, you will not be allowed to trade off services with other students. So, just be prepared." I surveyed my students. With the exception of footwear, they sat in front of me identically clothed, with nervous but attentive expressions on their faces.

The instructor, Ms. Davis, stood to the side as I rattled off the do's and don'ts: what happens if the students have unexcused absences; how their hours and minutes are accumulated and docked when they're late. It was our first official day of business and the first day of class. There were twenty-three students enrolled for this session but only nineteen actually showed up.

"You will get an hour for lunch and two ten-minute breaks. You must swipe your badges for all breaks as you do when you come in and leave for the day. That's the only way that your hours can be correctly calculated in the system. If you forget to clock in or out, let the office know immediately and the adjustment will be made. This adjustment can only be made three times during the nine months you're here, and will only be made if an instructor can vouch for you. Any questions?" I spoke to the group with one hand in the pocket of my slacks and the other resting on my tie. There was silence as all eyes focused on me. I looked around at the faces of my first students. I was a little nervous but played it cool.

"Well, if there aren't any questions, I will let Ms. Davis take over. Once again, welcome to Overland Park Cosmetology Academy." I motioned for Ms.

Davis to take the floor. Closing the door behind me, I stepped into my office and took a deep breath.

For years I'd dreamed of having my own school and successfully educating those who wanted to learn. My goal was to provide the best knowledge on hair care and hairstyling. I had hired some of the best instructors and trained them to give the students the kind of education they would be able to take with them anywhere.

I'd invited some top professionals from all around the country to come in and do classes on haircutting and coloring techniques. My graduates would be ready for anything and their capabilities would be endless.

I'd put years of work into getting this school off the ground, and there were still plenty of things to do. It was so funny how things worked out. Had Naomi accepted my proposal, I would've had the responsibility of trying to keep a wife satisfied and fulfilled while trying to get the school off to a good start. It was nice to think it could've worked, but I realized how difficult it would've been. Naomi required a lot of attention, which was part of the reason we didn't make it the first time.

Back then I couldn't give her the time she needed because of all of the other women I was seeing at the same time. And once she saw that I wouldn't cut all ties with them, she jetted, and did so without looking back.

Naomi and I were never ready for each other at the same time. She wanted me, and I wasn't interested. I finally got it together, and she didn't trust me. Now, it seemed she was doing everything she could to win me back. But I wasn't having it.

It wasn't that I didn't still love her. She is the only woman I've *ever* loved. But because of that, she had also done something no other woman had been able to do—she hurt me. And part of me wanted her to suffer the way I'd suffered.

When I woke up this morning, I discovered a voice mail message from Naomi wishing me well on the first day of class, and when I arrived to the school, there was a large hibiscus tree, which had been delivered to my office from her salon. I believed the effort Naomi was making to be sincere, and I appreciated the gesture, but the timing was all wrong. I wasn't ready to forgive her yet, and she just didn't get it. I sat at my desk and shuffled through the messages, trying to decide in which order I needed to return calls. Then I remembered all of the orders that needed to be placed to get the dispensary fully stocked and ready for the students when they got to the demonstration floor. It was going to be easier to move on with my day after I got the call to Naomi out of the way.

A young girl's voice came in over the speaker. "Good morning, Black Beauty. How can I assist you?"

"May I speak with Naomi, please?"

"Is this concerning an appointment?"

"No. You can tell her it's Wendell."

"Okay, just a moment."

"Hi, Wendell," Naomi said a moment later.

"Hey, Naomi. How are you?"

"I'm fine. How is everything going on your first day?"

"Pretty smooth, actually."

"Great." I could tell she was smiling. Naomi could be loving and sweet when she wanted to be. When she wasn't threatened by the presence of another female, she was a different person. "I just wanted to thank you for the plant. That was real nice."

"You're welcome. I hope it's not too big... for your office, I mean. I didn't know how much space you had, but was hoping you could find room for it somewhere."

"It's pretty big, but it looks great in here."

"I'm glad you like it."

"How are the kids?"

"They're fine."

"Good. Well, I've got some business to tend to, and I'm sure you're busy, too. Just wanted to say thanks."

"I really do wish you much success, Wendell. Really."

"I know." There was an awkward silence. "I'll give you a call later. Okay?"

"Okay. Have a good day."

I hung up the phone wondering why I'd promised to call her. I wanted to cut ties completely but I couldn't—or didn't know how. Cutting ties with women was something that had been so easy in the past. I just dropped out of sight, stopped calling, and ignored calls. It was simple. But, because of Sydney, I couldn't do that. I was forced to communicate with Naomi. And every time I had contact with her, I felt those familiar urges again. Habit and human nature made it difficult not to cross the line with her. She was still the woman I fantasized about. She was the one I dreamed of at night.

I couldn't let her know it. I wouldn't be calling Naomi back. In fact, she wouldn't hear from me until I went back to Wichita to visit Sydney. I had way too much on my plate for the time being. If she could go a while without creating drama, maybe we could hook up again. Maybe.

Chapter 9 *Glory*

...one headache that I should've avoided.

"*...and* when I tell y'all he did me wrong, *I mean wrong.* I don' went wit' drug dealers, gangsters, crooks, and criminals. But ain't nobody done me as bad as that preacher I was goin' wit'. I mean he to' my behind up."

The whole salon burst out in laughter. I wanted to laugh, too, but what I wanted more was for Ms. Millie to shut up. She was an attractive, older woman. Big and brown, with an even bigger mouth that was constantly going. But, this wasn't Showtime at the Apollo. I never liked it when clients, or hairstylists for that matter, used salon time for social hour. But we'd all grown accustomed to Ms Millie and what I referred to as the "Ms. Millie Show," every third Saturday of the month. She was one of Joyce's long-time clients who had the habit of entertaining everybody when she came in for her monthly appointment.

Joyce thought it was okay for clients to come to the shop to visit and socialize, and she had condoned that type of behavior, turning the salon into a meeting place of sorts. But even though she was laughing right along with everyone else, I knew she secretly wished for the episode to come to an end. But there was really no way around it. If we had asked Ms. Millie to stop, we would've felt far worse about hurting her feelings than we did sitting through her monthly vaudeville show. So, we all just laughed and went with it.

"Hey, Glo. Whatever happened to Stephanie?" one of Sweetie's clients asked me, once Ms. Millie had reclined for her shampoo and things had quieted down somewhat. "I haven't seen her in here in a long time? Did she change her appointment day?"

I didn't know whether to tell the truth, or try and avoid more questions by lying. Sweetie, in her own world, didn't even look up. She was obviously preoccupied with her own crap. So, I decided to slip in a misleading response.

"I guess y'all just been missing each other." I mumbled quickly, and walked off. I didn't really care if people knew that Stephanie was no longer my client, but if they knew they would wonder why. Stephanie was a permanent fixture here at the shop. If I said I was no longer doing her hair, I would have to tell the whole story or sit back while they made up their own versions of what happened, making it worse than whatever the truth really was.

Of course, a no-good man was behind it all. I'd known Gerald Warren for a couple of years and we'd been nothing more than passing acquaintances. His ex-wife, Marcia, was Stephanie's cousin, so Gerald and I frequently ran into each other at different functions and parties by way of Stephanie.

When he first asked me out after their divorce, I gave him the 'I'm not looking to get involved in a serious relationship' speech. The same speech I gave everybody. He claimed he was fine with that, but I should've known better than to hook up with a man who was just learning to adjust to the dating scene. He turned out to be a walking emotional wreck. He tried to play it cool at first, and I bought it for a minute, but as it would happen, he was looking for a replacement for his wife. He, unfortunately, had not made the adjustment from married-life into single-life.

Gerald was definitely one headache I should've avoided. Common sense told me that he wouldn't be stable enough to deal with a woman like me; I should've just passed. Getting involved with him also caused uneasiness between Stephanie and me.

Stephanie was not only one of my Friday morning regulars for eight years or so, but she was my really close friend. She felt awful because prior to Gerald and his wife's divorce, she'd disclosed some of their personal business to me during her visits to the salon, never thinking I would end up dating the man. When Gerald and I got together, her cousin thought Stephanie hooked us up. It wasn't for me to say, but Stephanie learned a good lesson about discussing other people's business.

Truth be told, I've always been attracted to Gerald. He was older, nice-looking, and represented the kind of man that the average woman would love the chance to be with. He and Marcia were both linked with all of the societal groups and clubs in the city. In fact, their divorce was major talk all over town. He, a corporate attorney, and she, a local real estate tycoon, both attended Howard University where they met and became engaged. They'd been married over twenty-five years when they finally split up.

One month into our rendezvous, or whatever you might call it, Gerald began flaunting me around his friends, family, and business associates. He took me on trips and bought me expensive gifts. I asked him if he was doing it to make Marcia jealous—not that I really cared—but he said no. He claimed that I appreciated the things he did for me and she never did.

Gerald enjoyed showing me off and he thought that all of those things he did for me was what kept me around. And he was right. Because even after he started tripping, I took my sweet time letting him go. I was trying to hang in there until after the trip to Cancun we were planning. For six months I put up with him carting me around as if I were a showpiece. He was showing me off like a brand new, red-hot Maserati.

The real tragedy was that I lost my friend and client. Stephanie and I were still friends, so to speak, but it would never be as it was before. Once the whole city began talking as if Gerald and I was a couple, Stephanie called me up the day before one of her regularly scheduled hair appointments.

"Glory, you got a minute? I need to talk to you." She sounded pissed.

"Yeah, let me change phones." I sensed I needed some privacy. I wasn't sure what she was going to say, but I knew the tension had been building surrounding the whole incident with her cousin. I went to the other side of the shop to the receptionist's desk.

"Okay, girl. What's going on?" I said, turning my back to Joyce and Sweetie.

"Glory, this thing between you and Gerald has put me in an awkward position with Marcia. Why are you doing this?"

"What does this have to do with you?"

"She's my cousin!"

"So what? Why is she holding what I do against you? You can't tell me who to see, just like you can't tell her who to see."

"That's not the point, Glo," she said.

"Then what is?"

"Don't play crazy. She has every reason to feel uncomfortable with me still coming to you to get my hair done."

"Why?"

"Because you're sleeping with her husband!"

"*Ex*-husband."

"You know what I mean."

"What is it that you want me to do? Stop seeing Gerald so she won't be uncomfortable? If Gerald wasn't seeing me he would be seeing someone else." I really didn't understand the problem.

"Why are you actin' as if you don't know what I'm talking about?"

"Look, I won't talk to you about him and you don't talk to me about her. How's that?"

Stephanie made an exasperated sound in the phone. "Let's just be real, girl. You are not seriously interested in Gerald. Glory, I have seen you go through men like a ho goes through condoms. In a couple of weeks—if not a couple of days—you are gonna be giving him the brush off."

"A ho. going through condoms, huh? That's an interesting analogy. Are you calling me a ho?"

"All I'm saying is that you have a new man every other week. And didn't you say you told him you weren't interested in a serious relationship? It's not worth all of this if you're just gonna mess around with him for a few weeks and then move on to the next man. What is he, twelve, thirteen years older than you? You are *hardly* interested in him."

"And that's *my* business. You *and* Marcia need to stay out of it."

Looking back on the whole incident, I should've thought it through and not been so selfish. I was fairly certain Gerald and I would not be together long-term, but I resented the fact Stephanie was trying to tell me who to date. At the time I just didn't see the connection between me dating Gerald and Marcia being her cousin.

"Glory, I really hate to do this, but if you're gonna keep seeing him I'm gonna have to stop coming to you."

"Are you serious?" I didn't see that coming.

"Yes, I'm serious!"

Stephanie and I had been friends for years and were practically family. We were thick as thieves, vacationing together and sharing secrets. She was close to my family and I was close to hers. I was there at the birth of her kids and they called me Aunt. They even came over to spend the night with me sometimes, just as my own nieces and nephews. Stephanie, in my opinion, was overreacting.

"Well, you do what you think is best. I'll talk to you later." I didn't even wait on her to respond and hung up on her. I was mad that she thought she could control me. What she was saying about Gerald and me was true. I knew the romance would be short-lived but I just didn't see why Stephanie had to involve herself in the equation.

At first I didn't think she was really going to leave me, go somewhere else, and actually sit in someone else's chair to get her hair done. Not only had she sworn by my skills as a hairstylist, but also by my Body Glo, Grow Back Conditioner. I created it especially for her and had cured the alopecia she'd suffered with for years. How could she just walk away?

Now there was this awkwardness between us whenever we ran into each other. The end of our client-stylist relationship was like a divorce. Our friends were split down the middle; the few who knew about the incident anyway. Friends in our circle who were also my clients weren't about to give up getting their hair done by me, so they sided with me and cut her off. And those who weren't my clients sided with Stephanie and started acting evasively towards me.

I missed her and knew she missed me because I'd heard through the grapevine she'd been chair hopping. Her hair looked a mess when I saw her last. But that was her choice, and besides I didn't know how to try and reconcile with her.

After Stephanie stopped coming in, I was determined to let Gerald stick around longer than I would have normally. We went everywhere together. Every concert, party, social function, or whatever was going on—we were there making an appearance.

What I didn't know was that Gerald thought we were on our way to holy matrimony because we spent so much time together. When I tried to cut him off, he lost it. That fool started following me, showing up at the shop, calling my family and phoning me all times of the day and night begging me to tell him why I wanted to end it. I was seconds away from getting a restraining order on him. This went on for weeks, and I heard he was still telling people we were together two months after the split. I guess he was embarrassed that he hadn't been able to hang on to me.

~~~

"Glory, I really likeded my hair last time. I ain't never really wo' my hair down like that. I always wear finger waves or a ponytail."

I turned my attention back to my client, Dyann, who was looking through a hairstyling book. She'd been occupying Stephanie's vacant appointment slot. She was around Frannie's age or younger, around five-foot three with huge breasts and a tiny waist.

"You want it like that again?" I asked, hoping it wouldn't take her as long to make up her mind as it did before.

"Naw. I want somethin' different. Umm, some finger waves or a freeze, maybe," Dyann said, looking up at me with the gold glistening from one of her two front teeth. Her over-exaggerated southern twang was kickin' in at first soprano. Every word she spoke was practically set to music. She was a very pretty woman with a beautiful head of auburn tinted hair, but ghetto-fabulous as hell.

"Dyann, remember I told you I don't do freezes and finger waves. Gurl, that stuff is dated anyway."

"Aw. I forgot. All you do is them booghee hair do's. Well, I did get a lot of compliments last time. Just fix it like your sister's. What's that called?"

"Like Sweetie's? Oh, it's just a dry wrap."

"Yeah. Her hair is pretty every time I come in. Yours too. That's cute what you wearin' too." Dyann looked me up and down, admiring my clothes. "Yeah. Fix it like that. When I get up enough nerve, I'm gon' get all my hair cut off like Ms. Joyce's hair ova there. Gurl, moms is lookin' like she could be y'all's sister." She watched my mother work.

"You could rock that, too." I was looking at Dyann and thinking, if she stuck it out with me long enough, I'd change her whole look. Down to the gold grill and the dragon-lady fingernails that were consistently polished with any and every color of the rainbow.

"All y'all so pretty," she said, looking over at Frannie and Sweetie." Did you use ta model or something'?"

"A little."

"Umm, really? I want my hair like yours next time." She settled into the hydraulic chair with a sense of satisfaction on her decision. "Next month I'm having a birthday party at the American Legion. So, I'm gon' need something special. Okaaay?"

"It would be cool if you softened your look by changing the kinds of hairstyles you wear." I also wanted to tell her to get rid of the accessories in her mouth along with changing the kind of clothes she wore. But we needed to take baby steps. There was a raving beauty underneath all of that excessive urban begging to be rescued. *When I am finished with her, she will be glossed and polished.*

Chapter 10 Frannie

...one less thing for me to be concerned with.

"Here. It's for you." I tossed Michael the ringing cordless phone with his deceased father's name displayed across the caller ID.

He fumbled with it several times before getting a secure grip. I walked out of the bedroom thanking God I had a mother who didn't feel the need to call our house ten times a day.

Mrs. Thomas had made it perfectly clear she was not happy with the choice her only son made for a wife. Several days into our new marriage, she confided in me that our wedding day had been the saddest day of her life. And sure enough, when the photos came back from the photographer, she was frowning in every picture.

A month later she pulled me aside following Sunday dinner to fill me in on the details of the 'nice young lady' she'd hoped would be her daughter-in-law. Michael's father overheard what she was saying and admonished her some. Unaffected, she pressed harder to convince me how much she adored the other girl. That's when I knew she was crazy.

"What did she want?"

Michael was placing the phone back in its cradle and I went straight to making up the bed. "She needs me to stop by when I get off work to move some stuff in the garage."

"Don't forget I'm working today, and you're picking up the kids."

"Oh. That's right. What time are you finishing up?"

"I don't know. I'm finishing up when I'm finished..." He knows how much I hate that question. A hairstylist can rarely determine the exact quitting time on any given workday. You never know what challenges may await. Someone is always needing more services than what they're scheduled for.

"...Which means you need to feed them. There's pork chops left over from yesterday, but you'll have to put some vegetables with them. Or you can go pick something up," I said and picked the comforter up and placed it back on the bed.

If I knew Michael, his mother would be feeding them. And I didn't really care because it'd be one less thing for me to be concerned with. It was just that she'd make sure I knew she fed my kids.

"They can just eat at Mother's."

"I figured as much."

We placed the pillows on the bed, and I walked toward the bathroom to take my shower. Michael caught me by the arm and moved in behind me. He left cold wet spots on my neck from his mouth and put his hands inside the neckline of my nightgown. We hadn't made love in weeks and just like before, I felt nothing. I froze up but he didn't seem to notice. His hands were all over me.

"Michael, I need to get in the shower."

"I'll get in with you." He breathed heavily in my ear.

The sound of Ericka crying crept through the partially opened door. I broke free from his embrace.

Michael grabbed my arm to stop me. "Let her cry."

"I really should check on her. She wasn't feeling well when I put her down last night."

"She'll be fine. Come here, baby."

Ericka's cry became louder and more insistent. It certainly didn't help set the mood for me, but he didn't seem to have a problem ignoring it.

"Let me at least peek in on her to make sure she's okay."

Michael began tugging at the buttons on my gown, totally disregarding what I was saying.

"Michael, stop."

"Damn, Francine. It's been weeks. If I didn't know better I'd think you were avoiding making love to me." He stepped back a little.

"What?" I re-buttoned myself. "I'll be right back."

I could see that he was crushed.

"I'll be back."

"Don't worry about it." His lips grazed my forehead. "Go ahead and check on the baby, and I'll jump in the shower." He pulled his undershirt over his head. "Get us a sitter for tonight, I'm taking you out." He disappeared into the bathroom.

I knew what he was thinking. My lack of interest in sex was somehow his fault and that he could fix it by doing something nice for me.

Ericka's cry had turned into an ear-piercing shriek by the time I made it down the hallway. And all I could think about was how did I explain to my husband that *I wasn't feelin' it*. My lack of libido had been a problem for longer than I cared to admit, and I didn't think that a night out on the town was going to repair what was broken.

It was a Friday at the salon, normally the kind of day we all liked. I was making plenty of money, catching up on what'd been going on with everyone since I'd worked last. Since I didn't work regularly it was a pleasant change from my normal day of doing wife/mother stuff. Joyce had cut back her hours, so today it was only us girls working.

"Sleepover at my house tonight," Glory announced while sweeping freshly cut hair. She got a big thrill out of having all the kids over. She loved her nieces and nephews dearly, and they loved her back.

"What time?" Sweetie asked from across the room, hot flat iron in hand.

"Anytime after eight. And Frannie you can send Ericka this time since Sydney will be there."

"My kids ain't coming," I said, standing over Tosha at the shampoo bowl.

Glory stopped sweeping. "Why not?"

"'Cause they're just not."

"Why you makin' Brandon and Little Michael miss out on the fun?" Sweetie asked. "You know my boys will tell them."

I didn't have an answer so I said nothing. How could I tell them I didn't want to be left alone with my husband when I couldn't even admit it to myself.

"Well?" Glory asked, still standing there holding the broom.

"Well, what?"

"What's the reason?"

"They have a basketball game in the morning."

"Just pack their uniforms—I'll take 'em. We can all get up and go to the game."

"Well, Ericka wasn't feeling well this morning so I should keep her home."

"She was feeling good enough for you to take her to day care," Glory said. She dismissed me with the flip of her hand and finished sweeping. "Well, whatever you decide."

Sweetie and Glory both gave me a, *What's wrong with you?* look but then they quickly moved on. I didn't want to talk about it anymore so that was good.

"Tosha, how are you wanting your hair styled?" I combed through her wet tangles as we faced the mirror.

"Just regular," she said, trying to find where she'd left off in her magazine.

"Regular what?"

"You know. Just like, regular."

"Umm. No, I don't know."

"Well, like you did it last time."

"I don't really remember what I did last time."

"It was *just* six weeks ago," Tosha said, with a little attitude mixed in with some airhead.

I could understand her thinking I should remember if I had done her hair last week, or maybe even two weeks ago. *But six weeks?*

"*Just?* You do realize that I've done plenty of people in between the time that you were here last."

Tosha looked at me in the mirror with an expression that clearly said she didn't get it. I could see that we weren't getting anywhere with the way that conversation was going, and decided that arguing with her was more trouble than it was worth. "Alright, girl. I know what you want." She was only my third client for the day and I was already totally fatigued and not really feeling well. Since she wouldn't tell me what she wanted I was giving her what I felt like doing. Blown dry and bumped under. She had too much damn hair anyway.

"Michael's on the phone for you, Frannie." Sweetie laid the cordless phone on my counter.

"Excuse me, Tosha."

I walked to the back room and took a deep breath before picking up. "Hello."

"Hey, Baby."

"Hey."

"How you feeling?"

"Okay."

"You think one of your sisters will watch the kids tonight? I thought we could go out. Maybe dinner or something."

"Umm. I doubt it."

"Just ask and see."

"Michael, I'm already tired and I'm sure by tonight I won't feel like going out."

"I just thought that we could use some time alone—we don't have to go out."

"I don't feel like packing for them."

"Frannie, are we okay?" He almost sounded afraid.

"Michael, I'm just tired."

"Okay. Well, we can stay in. I'll call my mother and see if the kids can go over there."

"No! Don't—Michael, let me call you back."

...that was how we did it in the Parker family.

"Mama, I'm here," Sweetie said, coming in through the side door.

I asked her to come by and touch up my color once she got the boys off to school. Monday was usually the day we did our own hair, and once I saw that ponytail of hers hanging out of the back of a baseball cap I knew getting a shampoo was on her mind also.

All of the struggles of raising my children and the ups and downs of single parenting notwith-standing, I was very pleased with the relationships I had with my children individually. Wendell was my heart. My firstborn. And there was always a special connection between a mother and son. There had been some rough times raising him, but there had always been a mutual love and respect between us.

Glory and I battled and had our mother-daughter issues but unbeknownst to her, I understood her and held an appreciation for her personality. Once she became a woman we acquired a fondness for each other that surprised us both.

Frannie never gave me a moment's trouble. Well, with the exception of when she was fighting with Glory. She handled her business and required very little from me. She never carried on, as one would expect the baby of the family to. And that could be due to Sweetie filling that role.

That girl was always underfoot. Sweetie clung to my skirt for so long I didn't think she would ever let go. She wouldn't talk to anyone outside the family until she went to kindergarten, and she didn't put together one full sentence for us until Frannie began talking circles around her. Before Frannie encouraged her to speak up, I was really the only one she spoke in front of. In fact she's the only one of my children ever to call me *Mama*. I'm not really sure how being called Joyce by the others all started. I believe when Wendell was small he heard so many others call me by my name he just repeated what he'd heard. And me being so young and inexperienced as a mother I never corrected it. And the others followed his lead.

"What you got to eat?"

"You didn't cook breakfast this morning?"

"No. The boys made themselves cereal. I kind of overslept."

I just shook my head. Now, she hadn't fed her own kids but came over for me to feed her? Yeah, she was my baby.

"I didn't fix anything this morning but there's some left over coffee cake I baked yesterday," I said. "Oh, and some coffee. I'll be waiting on you in the shop. Hurry up, girl."

~~~

The telephone was ringing non-stop while Sweetie applied hair bleach to my new-growth. Between playing receptionist I was inspecting and correcting her work. It wasn't that I didn't think she knew what she's doing, it was just that Sweetie had been known to leave holidays scattered throughout my hairline.

"Good morning. Joyce speaking."

"Hello. Ms. Parker, this is Naomi. How are you?"

"I'm fine, Naomi. How are you?"

"Well, I've been trying to locate Wendell. Have you heard from him today?"

"No, I haven't. Are you okay?" Naomi was breathing heavily and sounded upset.

"No. I'm not. I'm on my way to the school."

"Is Sydney sick?"

"No, she's not sick but something's going on. The principal just called. Wendell is supposed to be coming to town today, and I've been calling his phone all morning but it keeps going straight to voice mail. You haven't heard from him?"

"No. I didn't even know he was on his way here. Do you need me to come to the school?"

"Well... no... I don't know. Why don't I call you back after I find out what's going on."

"Okay. You call me back, ya here?"

"I will."

"Sweetie, rinse this out," I said as I hung up the phone. "We need to go up to Sydney's school."

"What's wrong?" Glory asked, coming through the door in sweats and a wool cap pulled down to her eyebrows. A matted ponytail hung down past her butt.

"I don't know. Naomi just called sounding upset and on her way to the school. She didn't say what was wrong." I leaned back into the shampoo bowl so Sweetie could rinse me. "She's trying to reach Wendell. Have you heard from him?"

"No. Not lately."

In a matter of minutes we were piled into Glory's car and on our way. Naomi didn't leave me with any hint as to what was going on at the school, so we were going there ready for whatever. We've made many of these trips on account of my children and my grandchildren over the years. This was just one more added to the list.

After trying to reach Wendell several times, Glory called Frannie to tell her to meet us at the school. Hopefully all of us showing up like this wouldn't startle Naomi, but that was how we did it in the Parker family.

Chapter 12 *Sweetie*

So, this is Naomi.

"*What's* going on, Naomi?" Mama was leading the pack that included my two sisters and myself. First Mama with her still slightly damp hair, then Glory looking like Russell from the Cosby Kids with a wool cap pulled down, Frannie acting exhausted with Ericka on her hip, and me bringing up the rear.

"Sydney was on a field trip and there was a problem with one of the parents," Naomi said, looking around as we filed in one at a time.

"Did you get in touch with Wendell?" Mama asked.

"I've left messages but he hasn't called back yet."

So this is Naomi, I thought to myself. I couldn't decide if the expression on her face was a reaction to all of us charging in, or whatever was going on with Sydney. We watched her huff and puff around the school's office as she waited for someone to give her an update.

I had never seen Naomi up close and personal like this. She looked mean, rude, and ready to cuss somebody out. I didn't expect her to be extra friendly and all smiles under to the circumstances but I did think she would at least be cordial enough to speak.

Rarely do we get to interact with any of Wendell's women. He never brought women around us—ever. The only time we found out about one of them was if they approached us, which wasn't often.

It figured that Wendell would fall in love with a woman like Naomi. Unlike every other female he was involved with, she seemed to be commanding, demanding, and a few other things I wouldn't mention.

Suddenly, it all made sense. Wendell was about thirteen, which made me about nine. It was a spring night and there was a thunderstorm brewing, complete with flashes of light and crashing thunder. I awakened and was on my way to Mama's room to see if she would let me sleep with her. When I got to her door, I could hear her on the phone. Her tone was different, which made me stop before entering. She told us to never use the telephone when the weather was like that, but there she was with the receiver up to her ear.

Mama was talking to Sister Sims, saying things that caught me off guard. I'd heard the rumors like everyone else that Mama was seeing Rev. Sims but this conversation was about Wendell. Mama asked Sister Sims if she was sleeping with Wendell to pay her and Jerome back. It was my first time hearing Rev. Sims' first name. It was also my first time hearing the word pedophile, and throughout the conversation I figured out what my mother was implying when she used it.

With a few other choice words, Mama ended the conversation with the threat to call the police if she didn't stay away from Wendell. When she hung up, I could hear her crying, so I knew it wasn't the best time to disturb her. I went back to my bed and prayed that Wendell wasn't in any trouble. Ever since that night I hated the sight of Sister Sims because that was the night things changed.

Wendell no longer had to go to church with us. Frannie kept insisting on knowing why, and Mama would tell her to mind her business. I kept my mouth shut and was never aware of how much Glory knew. Shortly after that we began going to another church, but we never actually joined. And since we were getting older, Mama was less forceful about us attending regularly.

"We've left messages for him too. He'll show up," Mama said.

We all took seats while Naomi paced in the small office, getting madder by the minute. Through her anger, I could see a smooth golden complexion, a perfectly made face, and what appeared to be freshly done hair. She was more than striking—more than pretty.

I sat and waited for something to happen: Naomi cursing out the secretary; the other parent walking in; Glory saying something to make the situation worse. Between her and Glory, anything could've gone down, especially if Wendell didn't hurry up and get here.

Chapter 13 *Wendell*

I wasn't in the mood to over-think the situation...

As soon as I entered the city limits my phone signaled that I had messages. It was Naomi, sounding irritated and saying that she needed me to meet her at the school. Something about a problem with Sydney and another parent.

I'd never had to involve myself with this side of parenting, but I guess there's no time like the present. I headed in the direction of the school and called Naomi. She didn't pick up and I considered calling my mother, but I thought twice. You can't just call one person from my family without getting the whole crew.

I parked next to Naomi's BMW in the gravel lot and made my way to the front office. When I opened the door I found the entire Parker posse crowding the small, glass-encased room, with Naomi in the middle. How did my whole family beat me to the school?

Naomi looked exactly as she sounded in the messages she'd left—upset and frustrated. I could see her irritation was quickly turning to anger.

"Sydney's father is here now," Naomi said, towering over a small-framed, middle-aged, Latino woman.

I was always excited to see Naomi, but I never knew it until I actually did. Without my permission a sexual tension stirred deep inside of me. A beige terrycloth jogging suit that clearly was not meant for exercise casually draped her body and caressed every full and firm curve. Her eyes were bright with an expression of agitation and her glossed lips pouted. Despite the scowl on her face, she looked soft. At that moment I desperately wished things were different between us. All the way here I'd felt the anxiety, but when Naomi came within eyeshot it lessened. But knowing her like I did, that would be short lived.

"Why don't you both join me in my office." Ms. Ramirez was nervous and more than likely intimidated by the swarm of family taking up every available piece of free space in the cramped area. I was certain she intentionally separated us from my mother and sisters.

Naomi and I listened while Ms. Ramirez attempted to downplay an incident where another student's mother yelled at Sydney and snatched her by the arm while on a field trip. She made it clear that she wasn't present when this happened, but could call in Sydney's teacher to give us a better account of the details.

"Where is she?" Naomi asked.

"She's in class."

"No, the woman that put her hands on my daughter." Naomi leaned forward in her seat. *"Where is she?"*

"Oh. She's still on school grounds, I believe."

"Will she be joining this conference?" I asked. "I'm interested in hearing what possible reason she had for touching Sydney." I thought it only fair that she be there to defend herself, whatever little defense she may have had. My baby might not be an angel when I wasn't around, but I couldn't imagine her doing anything that would make another adult angry enough to put hands on her. The thought of some stranger touching my little girl made my blood boil, but I tried to keep it in check because I could see that Naomi was mad enough for the both of us.

"I think it'd be best if we scheduled that meeting at another time. To give everyone a chance to cool off, you know?" Ms. Ramirez found it difficult to meet our gaze when she answered my question.

Naomi stood. "This is as cool as I'm gon' get."

There was a small commotion outside the door and then it opened. Two police officers walked in and introduced themselves. That's when I understood the seriousness of the situation. The principal was watering down the incident because she knew if we really knew what had gone down, somebody would be getting dealt with.

I stood, joining Naomi. "I need you to pull Sydney out of class. I want to talk to her."

Ms. Ramirez picked up her phone. "Could you call Sydney Parker to the office? Or better yet, why don't you go and escort her."

While the three of us waited for Sydney to be brought from her classroom, Naomi and I had a conversation through mental telepathy and eye contact. I was saying that I couldn't believe this shit; she was saying that she wanted to whoop that bitch's ass.

When Sydney walked into the room, I asked the principal and the police officers for privacy. They reluctantly obliged. It had been several weeks since I'd seen her last and it looked as though she had grown a couple of inches. She'd also lost another one of her baby teeth in the front.

"Hi, baby." I picked her up and hugged her tightly.

"Hi, Daddy. What you doin' here? I seen Aunt Glo and Grandma Joyce out there."

"We're here to find out what happened on your field trip this morning."

"What do you mean?"

"Whose mother did you ride with going to the museum?" Naomi asked.

"Oh. That was Kelsey's mother, Mrs. Hughes." Sydney acted as though she could barely remember the incident.

"Kelsey? The same little girl you've been having problems with?"

"Um. Yeah."

"Well, what happened?"

"What do you mean?"

"Did something happen while you were at the museum today?" Naomi and I were becoming confused by Sydney's nonchalant attitude.

"Oh yeah! She started yelling and screaming at me. I don't even know why."

"You mean Kelsey's mother?"

"Yeah!"

"Did she grab you by the arm?" Naomi asked, her breath quickening.

I could see the tape replaying in Sydney's mind. "Yeah! She did. She grabbed my arm and I almost fell. And then—and then she poked me in my forehead. And she was saying to me 'you think you're so much' or something like that. And Mrs. Thatcher made me ride back to the school with her instead of with Mrs. Hughes..." Sydney was rambling on nonstop, giving details as they came back to her. I could see why they preferred not to put children on the witness stand to testify.

I knew that look on Naomi's face. She could be the sweetest, kindest woman until she'd been wronged, and then she was ready to go bodies with someone. She moved toward the door.

"Naomi, remember the police are out there." I took her by the arm.

"Well they better escort her to her car because if I see her..." She broke free from my grip and began pacing.

There was a knock and then my mother opened the door and put her head through.

"Can we come in?"

Joyce held the door while Glory, Sweetie, and Frannie marched into the principal's office. After I gave them a play-by-play of what had happened that morning during the field trip, they were demanding we have the meeting right then, too. As the women in my family became more agitated, I started to reason with the principal. Between Naomi and Glory, the whole incident could have easily turned ugly and out of control. Glory was another one that liked to fight first and ask questions later.

"You know what, I'll be here a couple of days," I said. "I agree with the principal—let's set the meeting up for tomorrow."

I watched Sydney, wide-eyed and taking in the whole scene. She didn't even know there was a problem until we showed up asking questions. *Kids.*

"Forget a meeting. File a police report and sue that crazy heifer for assault," Frannie said.

"Naw," Glory said, holding Sydney in her lap . She was getting heated up. "Sometimes you got to bring it to people in a language they understand. She like to snatch on folks, I say we snatch her a…"

Joyce was calm and still clutching her purse. "Naomi and Wendell are the parents here; they will decide what happens. Wendell is right, there needs to be some discussion between the parents after everyone has calmed down. And adults have a way of making a situation worse than it has to be." She turned to me. "Go ahead and schedule your meeting, and if you want us to come with you we will. But the two of you can probably handle it from here."

My mother was always the voice of reason.

"Just pay me back when you can."

Carl looked at the money I placed on the bar. "I came over here to get some things off my chest. I wasn't looking for a loan, man."

"I know that. But, I understand the struggles of being a single parent. Something always comes up when you got kids. Besides, I know you're good for it. You'd have my back if the situation were reversed." I didn't want to insult him, but after listening to his problems I couldn't help but offer him some assistance. Carl and I had been friends since high school, even though we were complete opposites. He was the type of brother who stayed in a long-term, committed relationship, while I ran through women left and right. He was madly in love with every girlfriend he ever had and devastated when things ended. He never understood why I couldn't be with just one, and I never understood how he could. Despite our different lifestyle choices, and even though he'd married young and became the family man, we still remained tight.

I called to check on him since I was in town, to get his thoughts on the situation with Sydney at the school. So, he stopped by to have a drink. We sat at the bar in my den for several hours swigging on Coronas I found at the back of the mini-fridge. The room was cluttered with empty boxes waiting on me to fill them as every piece of furniture and fixture sat still and undisturbed.

Carl and Detra's marriage had been rocky for about a year when she finally left him with the kids. He was too heartbroken to make her pay child support, so he was striving to make ends meet. He thought that if he played the nice guy, she'd return home. I told him I didn't understand his reasoning but truth be told, I would've probably reacted the same way.

"I don't know when I can pay you back." Carl was still looking at the stack of bills.

"That's alright. Just take care of your kids and keep ya head up."

Listening to him talk about how much he missed Detra had me wanting to call Naomi. And not just to talk to her about what had happened earlier. Living away in K.C. I did fine without a woman around, but the minute I was within close proximity of her I weakened.

Carl stood and slid ten one hundred dollar bills in the front pocket of his Levis. He adjusted the ball cap that he wore to cover up his need for a haircut and began moving toward the door.

As soon as Carl was out of the door I went straight to the phone. Naomi picked up on the second ring.

"What are you doing?" I asked.

"We just finished dinner and I'm cleaning the kitchen." I could hear water running in the background.

"Oh." I hesitated.

"Are you hungry? There's still plenty of food?"

"Actually, I *am* hungry."

"Come on by. I'll keep it warm for you."

"Maybe, you could come by here..." My thought process faded. Now, what was I really asking her to do? I wasn't in the mood to over-think the situation, so I just finished saying what was on my mind. "I'd like to see you."

"It would have to be later. I have to help Sydney with her spelling words and get her to bed. And D.J. hasn't made it in from practice yet."

"That's cool... If you feel like getting out." I could've gone to her place but I didn't want to involve the kids when I wasn't sure of my intentions.

"I'll call you when I'm on my way."

"Don't forget my plate."

She gave me a sweet, sexy laugh. "Alright."

It was going on ten o'clock when Naomi rang the doorbell. She crossed the threshold carrying a brown paper bag with handles. I smelled a powdery floral scent rising from her body when she walked by. She wore a jogging suit just like the one earlier, except this one was plush black velour.

"Something smells appetizing."

"It's seafood pasta." She set the bag down on the kitchen counter.

"I was talking about you."

"Of course you were," she said with a wink. She went to the sink and washed her hands.

I dusted off a bottle from the wine-rack above my refrigerator while she got a plate from the cabinet. We both busied ourselves, unsure of what this whole encounter would mean.

"My family showing up at the school like that didn't scare you, did it?"

"Well, it didn't scare me, but I wasn't sure what to expect." She dumped a steaming pile of pasta with white sauce, loaded with shrimp, scallops, and clams onto a plate. "But, I was definitely relieved to see you walk through those doors."

I carried two wine glasses and the bottle over to the table while she carefully stacked asparagus tips on the right side of my plate.

"You looked pretty pissed when I walked in, and I wasn't sure why."

I filled the goblets, sat down and waited to be served. Naomi placed the plate in front of me along with warm bread wrapped in foil.

"I think I was mostly mad at myself. I usually drive on field trips. But this morning I had a dentist appointment and didn't want to reschedule it. My first time not going on a field trip with Sydney, and this shit happens."

"It's not your fault, Naomi."

"You know that woman wouldn't have done that if I had been there." Naomi was getting angry all over again.

"Probably not, but you couldn't know that was gonna happen." I said a quick, almost subconscious blessing over my dinner and dug in.

"When I got home today, I pulled out the school directory and looked up that bitch's address."

I stopped chewing. "Please tell me you didn't go over there."

"I did. And it took everything within me not to go up to the door."

"Naomi." I shook my head and went back to grubbing.

"That reminds me, they've scheduled the meeting for tomorrow at one."

"Okay. You gonna be able to control yourself?"

"We'll see." Naomi took a sip of her wine.

"Thanks for the dinner. It's delicious."

"I can tell. You've barely come up for air."

"I was starving."

"Sorry I didn't have any dessert to bring you."

"Oh, you brought it." I gave her a devilish grin and poured more wine in our glasses. I was attempting to keep the mood light, but Naomi didn't seem to catch on. A serious look clouded her face.

"You know, being in love with someone that you can't have is painful," she said.

I thought for a moment before I spoke. "Naomi, everybody's got a story to tell. You think you're the only one that's had your heart broken?"

"Okay, I've broken your heart, you've broken mine. Let's stop all this hurting each other and work this thing out."

"If only life were that simple." I continued to eat.

"It can be."

"I'm digging what you've done with your hair." Instead of the two extremes of extra curly or bone straight her hair was soft and wavy. It gave her a more subdued look.

"Oh. So you're gonna change the subject." She laughed, but not as though she thought it was funny.

"Why have you never let me do your hair?"

"So I could be added to the long list of tramps you had laying back in your shampoo chair? Not hardly."

"Why my client's gotta be tramps?"

"I *know* you don't want me to answer that." She took another sip.

Then I laughed. For some twisted reason I enjoyed it when Naomi was jealous.

After I finished my meal we took our wine to the den and sat in front of the television. Immediately I embraced Naomi and slowly brought my lips to hers. My hands touched every part of her body and she was a willing participant. She had one hand at the nape of my neck and her other arm wrapped tightly around me while my hands caressed her full hips. Our movements were unhurried and gradual, as though they were pleasures we took advantage of daily.

I made a trail of kisses from her chin, down her neck, to the top of her breasts. Pulling my polo shirt over my head, I brought her to me as we made motions to continue. Naomi was straddling my lap when she began unbuckling my belt.

I froze.

I took a hold of her hands, closed my eyes, and rested the back of my head on the sofa.

"What's wrong?" she asked, in a raspy whisper.

I brought her hands forward and touched each palm to my lips, one at a time. She let out a long sigh and shifted her weight.

"You changed your mind, didn't you?" she asked.

I couldn't gather my thoughts. What was I doing? What was I doing to her?

Naomi got up, straightened out her clothes, and stood for several seconds looking at me. Our eyes locked in on each other's. I was expecting her to curse me out at any moment.

Instead, she sat down next to me, picked up the remote control, slid her feet underneath my thigh, and began channel surfing.

"What do you wanna watch?" she asked, as she clicked.

"Baby, I'm sorry."

"Nothing to be sorry about." She continued changing channels while watching the screen.

Was this the same Naomi? I went with it. If she wasn't going to big deal it, then neither was I. I gathered that she was trying to show me a different side of her, and I wanted her to know I noticed.

"Thanks for understanding."

She exhaled a long breath and gave me a reassuring look. Thanks to my past behavior, she and I both knew how unattractive desperation was, and I could tell she was trying to control her emotions. The way this whole thing was playing out was tugging at my heart, and I felt myself falling for Naomi all over again. I watched her with the remote control and I could see the little girl again—that sweetness that would rise up in her from time to time.

I leaned over and buried my head in the silky tresses flowing from her head. After a while, we dozed off in each other's arms.

Chapter 14 Glory

I couldn't even form my mouth to say it.

I looked through the crowd of people to locate Dyann, and just as I spotted her, she saw me and yelled out. The music was loud so I couldn't hear her, but I knew she was calling me over. She and some of her guests were all bunched together throwing back shots of tequila. Even from way across the room, I could tell they were all three sheets to the wind.

I walked into the American Legion, a small building sitting right at the edge of the hood. I'm not sure what the original intent of the place was when it was first built, but its basic use was as a night spot for those who wanted to do a little dancing and get bent on one and a half drinks. The Bouncin' Bucket, The French Quarters, Seasons, The Club Rendezvous, The Club International and it's sequel, The International II, were all clubs that had come and gone, but The Legion, as it was affectionately called, still stood.

I hadn't been in a couple of years, but I had some fond memories of nights when Sweetie and I, still underage, had snuck out to drink and dance. I used to spend a lot of time here, but it wasn't really my kind of place now. Back in the day, it was little more than a shack of a building. But now it'd been renovated and built onto several times. The low ceilings and two awkwardly-placed bars were just a couple of telltale signs of the many low-budget restorations.

It was a Sunday night, and Dyann obviously had a lot of friends and family that came out to celebrate with her. They seemed to be having fun, but I questioned whether or not I'd be able to blend in.

Sweetie and Ric were supposed to meet me, but I didn't see them. I asked Sweetie to go with me, but she couldn't seem to go anywhere without her man, which was so typical of her. Whenever she got a boyfriend, she acted as though he was the only thing that mattered in her life.

"Hey, gurl!" Dyann yelled out, waving me over again.

"Happy birthday." I handed her a card with a gift card to Bath & Body Works tucked inside, hoping she would go and get herself something nice and feminine to go along with the new look I had given her.

"You know, I didn't think you was comin'," she said over the music.

"I told you I would. I'm not sure how long I can stay, though." If Sweetie didn't show up, I was out.

"I want you to meet my family." Dyann took me by the hand. "Hey, y'all. This is Glo, my new beautician I was tellin' y'all 'bout." I hated being called a beautician. It sounded so *back-in-Joyce's-day*; she could've just said I was a friend.

Dyann's friends and family occupied six tables. Folks checked me out, but barely acknowledged my presence. There were quite a few women, with a man mixed in here and there. I sat down in a vacant chair and this chick with a horrifying bleach job leaned towards me.

"You do this girl's hair name Kim, don't you?" Her head was bobbing up and down and I couldn't tell if it was because she was affirming the answer to her own question, or if she was keeping time with the music.

"Kim who?"

"I don't know her last name. But, she work down at the jail."

I should've known that's the one she was speaking of, considering she looked as though she'd just made bail. "Oh, you're talking about Kim Hunter."

She hunched her shoulders. "I don't know. All I know is that her hair is always slammin' every time I see her."

"Ah, thanks."

"Uh huh, you the one that be making that hair grease and stuff."

"Yes, I make hair and skin products." I almost wished I had packed some free samples to pass along.

"Uh huh." She was still nodding her head.

I turned to Dyann. "What you drinkin'?"

"The bartender knows."

"Alright." I headed to the bar nearest me.

The bartender looked like Eddie Caine Jr., with a black bandana tied around his head Aunt Jemima style. "I need a drink for the birthday girl and a Coke with a splash of Courvoisier," I said.

A young guy stood beside me at the bar, waiting to order a drink. "Whassup?" he said.

"Hi." He was very cute, with a large firm body. His chocolate brown complexion was silky smooth, and he was maybe two years into his locs. Although his appearance told me he was way too many years my junior, he had this thing that held my attention. Or, maybe it was just because he was so damn fine.

"You here for Dyann's party?" he asked, in a rough voice.

"Yeah. Isn't everybody?"

"I guess." He checked me out. "You ain't lookin' like one of her girls."

"We haven't known each other long. I'm her hairstylist."

"Is that right?" He stepped back, giving me a thorough once over.

"What is all that for?" I asked.

"Aw, my bad." He chuckled.

Niggah.

The bartender set two drinks down in front of me. "Nine dollars," he told me. He turned to the black Adonis sportin' the locs while he waited on me to pay him. "What you need?"

"Pepsi or Coke. Whichever one you have."

I handed the bartender a twenty and turned back to the inquisitive cutie pie at my side. "How do you know Dyann?" I asked.

"We're cousins, but we grew up together like brother and sister."

"Oh, really." I waited on him to ask my name or something, but he didn't. The bartender laid my change on the counter. I slid him a couple singles, picked up the rest along with my drinks, and headed back to the gathering.

I couldn't wait to get a buzz going so I could deal with the head-banging music that blared through the speakers. Songs with offensive lyrics made it difficult to catch a groove for me. Because she was out on the dance floor, I placed Dyann's drink on the table and took a seat. Then I looked around the room for Sweetie again. No sign of her. After a while, Dyann came back to the table, sweating and obviously having the kind of birthday she'd set out to have. "Thanks, Glo."

I nodded and took another sip. If Sweetie and Ric weren't there by the time I finished my drink, I was out. Just as I was plotting my escape, a tall dark-skinned woman with her hair cut low walked over to Dyann and grabbed her behind.

"Hey, baby," Dyann said, as she reached up and locked lips with her. Shock was all over my face. I tried to change my expression, but couldn't. I just hoped no one was looking at me.

"This is Glo," Dyann said, when they finally came up for air. "She's the one that's doin' my hair now. Glo, this is Toni."

"Hey, how ya doin'?" I said as nonchalantly as I could, and then took another sip. Toni barely nodded and turned away.

As I finished my drink, I thought, *If I leave now, Dyann will think it's because she has a girlfriend.* She had to know that I didn't know until right then. Didn't she? Either way, I was stuck for a while. Damn, where the hell was Sweetie?

"You need another drink?" I turned to see Dyann's cousin sitting at the table behind me.

"I was thinking about it, but I'd better not. The drinks are so strong. I wasn't planning on staying long anyway..." I looked at him knowing I was rambling on and he smiled at me showing beautiful white teeth.

"You didn't know, did you?"

I batted my eyelashes and tried to look as innocent as possible. "Know what?"

"I saw your expression. You didn't know Dyann was gay."

I didn't know how to respond. If I said I knew, he would see through that. But, if I said I didn't know I wasn't sure how it would come out. He might think I was homophobic or judging her. Before I could think of the right thing to say, he started laughing.

"You should see your face right now," he said, jeering me.

"It just caught me off guard." I began laughing a little, too.

"I thought you were one of 'em, until just then."

"You thought *I* was..." I couldn't even form my mouth to say it. He started laughing again.

"What's your name, Ma?" he asked, scooting his chair in closer.

"Glory," I said, extending my hand to him.

He took it and said, "Glory, huh? That's beautiful. I'm RoShon. I was lookin' at you when we were standing at the bar thinkin', '*Day-um*.' Another one don' went to the other side."

"Glad we cleared that up." We both gave a hearty laugh.

"You wanna dance?"

"Yeah." I stood and my knees buckled from the effects of the Courvoisier.

RoShon took me by the arm. "You alright?"

"The drink was stronger than I thought." We walked out to the dance floor and I got an even better look at RoShon. He sported a five o'clock shadow on his face, dense, dark eyelashes, and a sparkle in his eyes. He was wearing a thick navy blue sweater, baggie jeans that were slightly sagging, and dark brown Tim's that were unlaced. He was damn sexy.

I didn't usually go for younger guys, but I never really ran into one that made me consider it either. Until now.

RoShon and I were swaying to the beat of the music, and after the third song came on, he came in close and put his mouth to my ear. "You threw off my whole plan this evening."

"How's that?"

"I was planning to shoot through to tell Dyann happy birthday, and then jet. I haven't kicked it in a club in a minute."

"Is that right?"

RoShon backed up and continued dancing to the beat of the music. I moved forward and put my mouth to his ear. "So, you're saying you stayed because of me?"

RoShon slowly looked me up and down, and then the slightest grin came across his face. He never answered my question, probably because he knew that I knew the answer. I could tell that he had much game. But I wasn't an amateur either.

When the song faded into another one, I tugged RoShon's arm to let him know I wanted to stop. He walked me back to the table and I put on my coat.

"I'm gonna head out," I said to RoShon. I walked over to Dyann who was being smothered by her he-woman lover to tell her goodnight.

"You leavin' already?" Dyann asked.

"Yeah. I need to get going."

"Alright, I'll walk you out." Toni tightened her grip around Dyann's shoulder.

"That's okay..." Looked as though it was gonna be a problem.

RoShon appeared at my side. "I got you," he said, slipping into a brown leather jacket. "You ready?"

We walked out onto the paved parking lot and I thought back on a time when it was once dirt and gravel.

I pointed in the direction of my car. "I'm over here."

"You sober enough to make it home?"

"Oh, yeah," I said, and then wondered what his response would've been had I said no. I was wishing I could've done that over.

RoShon started laughing again.

"What are you laughing at?"

"Your face—I can't get that expression you made out of my mind. You should've seen yourself, Ma." He held his stomach more out of gesture than necessity.

I lightly tapped him on the arm with my fist. I was digging RoShon's laugh and didn't mind him laughing at me. When we reached my car, I unlocked the door and sat in the driver's seat. I expected him to ask for my phone number or when he could see me again. But he didn't.

"Have a good night and be careful going home." He closed my door and gave me a small nod as he turned to go to his car. I sat there feeling the sting of his dis for a few seconds, and then started the car.

Chapter 15 Frannie

...the road I was headed down wasn't it.

I sat in my car for two hours crying. I knew it wasn't the worst thing in the world, but it sure felt like it. All I wanted from the doctor was some vitamins, or for her to give me some simple prognosis as to why I'd been so tired and uninterested in sex with my husband. Advice to cut back on work, or some Cialis or Viagra-like pills they must have for women was what I was expecting.

What a difference a couple of words could make. Of course, I was pregnant before Dr. Boyd gave me the news, but the difference was a couple of hours ago, I was none the wiser. If I could just have those moments back. Those moments of not knowing.

I went home to lie down and escape the whole situation for a while through sleep. But before I could close my eyes, Michael called to see how the visit with the doctor went. I don't know why, but I couldn't bring myself to tell him I was pregnant. I told him she gave me a prescription for some vitamins and told me to take it easy. It was technically the truth; I just didn't mention that the vitamins were prenatal. I let him know I was just about to fall asleep and then quickly got off of the phone.

I don't remember much after that because only moments later, I awoke to a loud ringing sound in my ears, and after several seconds I realized it was the telephone. I picked up the receiver and then dropped it on the night table.

"Hello," I finally said, after securing it in my hands.

"Mrs. Thomas?"

"Yes?"

"I'm calling from the school. Michael and Brandon are still waiting to be picked up. I have them here in the office. Will someone be along to get them?"

I glanced at the clock—it was thirty minutes past time for me to have picked up the boys. "Oh! I'm so sorry. I'm not feeling well and I overslept." I looked around the room for my purse. "I'll be right there. Tell them I'm on my way."

With my mind still hazy, I moved as fast as I could to the garage and sat in the car while I tried gathering my strength. I was dizzy and weak, but knew I had to get going because not only was I late getting the boys from school, I was late picking Ericka up from daycare. She should've been picked up more than an hour ago.

I drove slowly and carefully, feeling like a drunk driver. In the middle of my trip I realized that I was really in no shape to be behind the wheel of a car. I should've called one of my sisters to help me out. I didn't want to call Michael because I wasn't ready to tell him what was really going on.

"Mama! Mama! Where were you?" Brandon yelled as he ran to me. His older brother stood behind him looking worried as I entered the school office.

"I'm sorry, boys. I lost track of time."

One of the school secretaries was standing in front of the desk with her purse on her shoulder, obviously a little more than aggravated.

"Were you the one that called? I'm so sorry."

I wasn't sure if she accepted my apology but I didn't have the strength of mind to care.

"Thank you so much for waiting with them. It won't happen again."

"That's okay." She began looking a little concerned. "Are you alright?"

"Just feeling lightheaded. I'll be fine."

"Do you need to sit down for a minute?" She looked me up and down.

"No. We don't have that far to go."

The boys gathered up their things and Mikie picked up a cage with two little furry creatures moving around in it.

"Michael, what is this?"

"Remember, it's my turn to bring home the hamsters for the weekend. *You said I could.*"

"Hamsters—I guess I forgot."

"You're not gonna make me leave 'em, are you?"

"No. Just come on."

We followed the secretary out of the building and piled into the mini-van. I sat behind the steering wheel still trying to gather strength.

"Where do you want me to put the cage, Mama?"

"Just sit it down on the floor," I answered. With my head leaning back against the headrest, my stomach began to churn and my mouth watered.

I could hear a small ruckus coming from the back seat. Brandon asked Mikie what he was doing, and a small exchange between the two went on for several seconds while I waited for my nausea to subside. I had just opened the door when the lining of my stomach came up and Mikie announced that one of the hamsters had gotten out of the cage.

They scrambled around on the floor as I sat there miserable. I knew if the hamster showed its face in the front seat I was going to pass out. What was I thinking when I said it was okay to bring those damn things into my house? We hadn't even gotten off school grounds and one of them was already out of the cage. With all the school papers, sports equipment, and whatever else littering the floor of the backseat, it was possible the hamster would be long dead by the time we found it.

"Y'all better find that thing and get it back in the cage."

Brandon let out a loud scream and began crying.

"What the hell is going on back there?" I demanded.

"The hamster bit me!"

"Oh, damn! Are you bleeding?"

"Yes!" He continued to cry.

"Did you get it in the cage?"

"No."

"I'll catch it," Mikie said.

"Somebody better catch it."

I started the engine and headed toward the Immediate Care Center to get Brandon checked out. They were still down on the floor as I drove down the street. I know I should've made them get back in their seatbelts before taking off, but I wanted that little fur ball back where it belonged. I felt around inside my purse for my cell phone but couldn't find it. I needed to let Michael know he would have to pick up the baby.

"Ouch!" Mikie yelled out.

"What happened, now?"

"The hamster bit me, too. But, I'm not gon' cry, Mama."

"Oh, damn."

I sped down the street and looked on the floor near my feet to make sure the little thing hadn't joined me up front. Then I glanced at the floor on the passenger side and there it was, its beady eyes looking up at me.

"It's up here!" I yelled.

"I'll get it!" Mikie dove between the seats up to the front while Brandon continued to cry in the back.

"No. Just leave it. I don't want it biting you again."

A siren wailed in back of me, and I looked up at the rearview mirror to see an officer motioning for me to pull over.

There was no time to tell them to get buckled in so I just pulled over to the side of the road. The officer said he stopped me because my vehicle was swerving, and gave me a ticket for reckless driving, not wearing a seatbelt, and not having my children secure in safety restraints. He said that Brandon was small enough that he should have some sort of child seat, so that was another citation. He didn't care that there was a hamster running loose in the car and that my son was bleeding all over the backseat and needed medical attention.

The officer wrote the ticket up and handed it to me. I didn't even care. We all put on our seatbelts and continued on our way with the hamster still loose in the van. And we left his little ass loose while we were in the clinic.

Two tetanus shots—one for each of the boys—and two band-aids later, we were on our way. It was seven o'clock in the evening when I thought about Ericka again. The daycare closed at six-thirty and they had expensive late fees. Ten dollars a minute or some crazy shit like that. I drove by there, and when I saw it was deserted, I hoped Michael had gotten her.

We pulled into the driveway and Michael was sitting in a lawn chair inside the garage next to his truck, holding Ericka. I couldn't tell if he was worried or angry. Instantly, I began feeling nauseous again.

"Francine, where have you been?" he asked me, before we could even get out of the van. "I've been calling your—" He opened my door when I stopped the car.

I didn't say a word. I rushed past him and made my way to the bathroom just off of the kitchen. I could hear the boys telling him about the hamster and them getting bit and the trip to the doctor.

Seconds later Michael was knocking on the bathroom door, calling my name. I flushed the toilet and took a look at myself in the mirror. My hair was smashed in on one side of my head, obviously from the nap I took hours before, and when I looked down at the wrinkles in my clothes, I noticed for the first time that I was wearing two different shoes.

I'll be damned. No wonder I had been getting so many crazy looks. I felt like shit and looked like it, too. I splashed some water on my face and took a slow, deep breath. If Michael didn't stop knocking on the door I was going to lose it.

"Francine!" he yelled, still knocking.

"Stop knocking on the door like a fucking crazy person!"

I didn't need to see his face to know he was in shock. I had never spoken to him or anyone else for that matter, that way before. Well, except maybe Glory.

Michael lowered his voice. "I'm sorry, baby. Are you okay?"

"I have diarrhea. Can I please have some privacy?" That would get him away from the door.

"Aw—okay. I'll go and get the Immodium."

"What you can do is help those boys find that damn hamster."

I stayed locked in the bathroom with my back up against the door for nearly an hour, listening to what was going on around the house. One of the boys made an attempt to come and get me, but before he could knock I heard Michael telling him to get away from the door and leave me alone until I came out.

What was I going to do with another child running around this house? This was not at all what I had in mind for my life. I wasn't sure exactly *what* I wanted, but I knew the road I was headed down wasn't it. Ericka had just turned a year old. Being pregnant again so soon was embarrassing to say the least, but more than that, it was exhausting to even think about it.

I finally emerged from the bathroom and found Michael on the sofa in the den, already nodding off to sleep. Brandon and Ericka were on the floor playing, but not with each other, and Mikie was at the counter looking at the hamsters in their cage. I nudged Michael on his leg until he opened his eyes.

"You need to watch the kids. I'm lying down."

"Oh—okay. What are you cooking for dinner?"

"What?"

"What are we supposed to eat?"

Instead of answering him, I let out a long breath and walked away.

Chapter 16 Joyce

Those were the words crowding my mouth...

"*Um,* these booth rent receipts don't really add up the way they should, Joyce," Ella said, reluctant to deliver the news via telephone. "They seem to be short."

"Probably because Sanita missed paying a couple of weeks last year."

"It's more than a couple weeks missing here." I imagined her holding up her adding machine tape looking over the tops of her wire-framed bifocals inspecting the figures. Ella Evans of Evans Tax Service had been preparing my income taxes since I got started in the business and I didn't dare think of trusting anyone else.

"I didn't mean a couple, literally. That was just a figure of speech."

"Well, there is some pleasant news. You can write it off and the truth is you have more deductions this year than you did last year even though your income was about the same."

"Meaning?"

"Meaning maybe a decent refund this year. But let me finish calculating and I'll get back with you when I'm finished."

I sat on my stool holding the wooden handle of a smoking-hot pressing comb with a dab of grease on the back of my hand. Ella still got an old-fashioned press and curl; complete with Hair Rep just like her mother who sat in front of me holding onto her ears as I made my way around her edges.

"Did all my girls get their stuff in to you?" I switched the phone to my other ear as Frannie walked through the door.

"I've already finished Glory's, and Frannie called and said that she would be getting all of her and Michael's paperwork from their plumbing business to me by the end of the week. And you know Sanita; I'll probably be filing an extension for her like I do every year."

"I know. Procrastination is that girl's middle name. She'll probably owe the IRS both of her kids before it's all over with."

"Joyce, you crazy." Ella laughed, but I didn't.

Sweetie was forever bringing up the rear at tax time. I stayed on her because I knew if it weren't for me she'd be in some serious trouble with the government. One year she filed an extension in April, then again in August and when that deadline rolled around, on October 15th, she was running to the mailbox to get her tax return postmarked before midnight. She had the worst business sense of all of my girls.

I'd been adamant with Wendell and the girls about being on the up and up with Uncle Sam. I worked for many years with others in the industry that did everything they could to get around it. They refused to take checks believing they could be tracked as income, refused to open bank accounts and if they worked for commission, they only stayed at salons that would pay them under the table. I knew so many of them that worked for years without reporting any income only to have it come back and bite them on the behind later when they couldn't collect social security.

"How much longer on Mother's hair?" Ella asked.

"Give me another thirty minutes or so and she'll be ready to go."

"Okay. See you in a bit."

This was the time of year that brought out the worst in us Parker women. After so many years, we should be used to it, but we all got grouchy when the time came to start gathering receipts and compiling deductions, not to mention sometimes sending in big checks. But life was good, and so was business.

I watched Frannie walk over to her work area and start to rummage through her drawers. She was stuffing receipts into a large manila envelope. Her expression was sour and stressed. We expected Sweetie to be a little irritable around this time of year so I was surprised when Frannie appeared to be the one letting tax time get to her.

"What's wrong with you slamming things around over there?" I asked Frannie.

"Oh. Sorry, I'm just tired, I guess." She walked over with her envelope stuffed to the brim. "I got what I came for. Do y'all need something 'fore I go?"

I looked Frannie in the face. "Are you okay?" And there I saw it.

"Just tired." She looked back at me.

"Oh Lord. Children are a blessing from God."

"Huh?" she asked indignantly.

I shook my head and said, "Just turn on the light in the front when you leave, please."

"Okay." She walked out as if her body weighed a thousand pounds.

Before I could even focus on what was going on with Frannie, my mother started up this nasty habit of hers of offering advice that always ended up hurting someone's feelings.

"Glory, when you gon' settle down, baby? Get you a man to take care of you."

"Grandma, don't start that today," Glory said, shaking her head.

"I just don't want to see you mess yo' self up like Sweetie." My mother was speaking as though Sweetie wasn't standing less than five feet away from her.

"Both of you are beautiful girls but not even a good man wants a woman with a bunch of somebody else's kids. You ain't had no babies, so that makes you a catch, girl." The sound of her voice was so sweet and gentle, to someone who didn't know better, it sounded as if she were handing out heartfelt compliments. But we all knew better.

I loved my mother but she had never done anything to help unify our family. All she did was break it down. She sat in Glory's chair across the room getting her weekly 'do. Every Wednesday we passed her around like an old family heirloom. Although there were times I failed to see her as a treasure, she still had given me life so I did my best to respect her.

"Just ask your mother. Joyce knows don't no man want a woman with kids."

"I don't know any such thing," I said. "Glory, you live your own life. If you ever want my advice, I'll give it to you but you do what's best for you."

"I will. And being some man's doormat ain't in my plans."

"A woman needs a man to take care of her, I don't care what you young people think. Times haven't changed that much," Mother said.

"Then, why haven't you remarried?" Glory asked.

"I was busy raising my children. And, I'm too old now."

Raising her children? Is that what she called it? Showing favoritism, creating dissension between my brothers and sister? Please. I wasn't nearly as angry or bitter as I could've been or maybe even should've been. And I didn't so much mind her talking about me having children without fathers. But I wouldn't stand for her talking about my daughters.

"See, Frannie did it the right way. She got herself a good man and don't have to worry about a thing."

"Mama, don't do that. Don't compare my girls with each other."

"I'm just trying to help so they don't repeat the cycle. I'm too late with Sweetie but it's still a chance with Glo if she don't mess up."

I didn't like making scenes in front of our clients so I kept quiet. How did she feel qualified to give advice when she had one son who had spent the prime of his life in prison, a gay son who couldn't stand her to the point he won't even mention her by name? And her daughter who she invested all of her time and energy into tolerated her only when she had nothing better to do. I was the only one—the one she all but threw away—that tended to her and made sure she had what she needed, along with my bastard children. *We* took care of her. Those were the words crowding my mouth. But, those words would never be released.

Chapter 17 Sweetie

That was always the process.

Hustler's withdrawal was what they called it. And before I figured out what was wrong with Ric, I was sure he was a drug addict. It was more the mood swings than anything else that convinced me he had some sort of an addiction. He didn't really fit the profile of what I thought someone on drugs looked like, but I didn't know what else to call it.

What I learned was, not only did the customer of a dealer have a habit, but also the dealer himself. His rush came from making large amounts of instant cash, and when he no longer had the influx of money coming in, he went through withdrawal just like any other addict. It had such a strong hold on him; he couldn't seem to let go of the profession or the lifestyle.

It was just like gambling, alcoholism, overeating, or any other thing people did that they couldn't control. The only difference was that what Ric was doing was illegal, not to mention the ugly stigma attached to it. Alcoholics and overeaters weren't demonized the way drug addicts and drug dealers were. Neither were gamblers or sex fiends for that matter. But an addiction was just that, and once it was defined, it had to be dealt with.

In order to overcome the addiction, Ric needed a substitute, and knowingly or not, he made me the replacement. But there were moments when even *I* wasn't enough to fill the void. He would fall into a depression and display erratic behavior like a junkie. At first I thought it was because he was a man and he didn't feel right about not going to work everyday. It was a while before I woke up to what was really going on. I got my first clue when I realized that financially, there didn't seem to be any changes. He was still taking care of my boys and me and over indulging us. Even I could do the math. If he was constantly spending and not making, the stash was going to dwindle.

Then one day, I made the mistake of suggesting he go and get a simple job until he got the thing with his security clearance worked out. He took it as an insult, flew into a tirade, and proceeded to tell me that I would never be interested in a man who stocked shelves overnight at a grocery store. Clearly I'd hit a sore spot, so I left it alone. But the more I thought about it, the more offended I got that he thought my interest in a man hinged on what he did for a living. I wanted to set him straight, but could see that mentally, he was not in a place to hear me. There were several occurrences where Ric showed the behavior of someone suffering from withdrawal. He spent money erratically and irresponsibly, became angry with me, and then would feel sad and dejected. That was always the process.

There was a time when the weekend was coming and Ric asked me to fly to L.A. with him just to get away. Under normal circumstances, I would have happily accepted. But, he was still minus a job and again, I was no mathematician, but I knew he couldn't possibly afford it.

"Why L.A.? What's going on there?"

"Nothing. I just want us to kick it for a couple of days." We sat across the table from each other at one of our favorite spots. His cold black hair glistened in the dim lights of the dining room, and his thin mustache perfectly framed his smooth, full lips. He cut into his steak and pink juices ran onto the plate.

"Ric, that's just blowing unnecessary money. Can you afford that?"

"What the hell you mean? I wouldn't offer if I couldn't afford it." He dropped his knife and fork onto the table.

"But you're not working."

"Sanita, don't ever try and count a niggah's money!" He pushed back from the table, stood, and walked away.

Ric was gone from the table long enough for me to complete my meal. I didn't know if he had abandoned me, or what. But then, he walked back to the table with a drink in his hand, acting as though nothing had happened.

"Hey, baby. How was your salmon?"

"Where were you?"

"I stepped outside to make a phone call."

"So, you just left me here at the table by myself?"

"I had business to take care of."

"I don't *even* want to know what that means." I folded my napkin and placed it on the table. "Are you eating your steak or sending it back?"

"Fuck it. I lost my appetite looking at that raw shit." Rick threw five twenties on the table, downed his drink, and stood again. "Let's go."

Growing up in the Parker family, we were never allowed to waste food. It was killing me to leave it behind. I visualized my boys fighting over that steak when I walked through the door.

"I can't leave all that for them to just throw away." I caught the attention of a passing waiter. "Excuse me, can you box this up for us, please?"

"I said let's go." Ric's voice was low and controlled. He took me by the hand and led me out the door.

On the way home he laughed and joked as if everything was cool, while my mind was back at the table with the food that was getting thrown out. Maybe he had gotten some good news while he was on the phone, but if it didn't have anything to do with a job, then it wouldn't be good news to me.

Around 11:30 P.M., Ric dropped me off at home saying he needed to make a run and would be back in an hour. I didn't see or hear from him until the next evening. When he called he sounded fine, but by the time he actually made it over, he was quiet and despondent. I learned not to ask him about his mood swings and he didn't offer much by way of conversation. It was clear to me: all was not fine.

Chapter 18 *Wendell*

...shouldn't take us long to come to a conclusion.

"I'll be coming home this weekend for Sweetie's birthday dinner. You could ride back with me on Monday, speak to the class on Tuesday, and I'll fly you back to Wichita that evening. How does that sound?"

"Sounds like it could work. What would you like me to speak to the class about?"

"Let's see... I know you're an excellent colorist, but I've already had someone come in and speak on hair color. Why don't you do a class on running a salon, or what it will be like once they graduate and get into the workforce?" Naomi and I had been playing phone tag all day long. I finally reached her to see if she would come lecture my students. I didn't think she was really feeling it at first, but I knew she was interested in spending time with me.

"That *would* be a good weekend. I just need to find something to do with Sydney. D.J. can stay home by himself for a few nights, but..."

"Well, let me know. I'm sure Glo would watch her if you needed her to."

"Okay, I'll have the logistics figured out by the end of the week. But count me in."

"All right. Hey? You in the bed?"

"Yeah, I'm getting in now." I could hear covers rustling in the background.

"Umm. What you wearin'?" I asked in my best Barry White.

"Wendell, you're crazy. Goodnight."

"Girl, I ain't playing. What you got on?"

"Goodnight." Naomi hung up the phone. I guess she really thought I was joking around. That's all right. I used my imagination accompanied by memory.

Being in love with Naomi had never been the question; I just needed to decide what I was going to do about it. Once I decided that I needed to reconsider making things work with her, it literally was like a ton of bricks hitting me all at once. But unlike last time, I knew not to jump in headfirst, and promised myself that I'd move slowly. She and I both needed time to heal and get reacquainted. I didn't want to repeat my past mistakes and I was sure she felt the same way.

The time we spent together in K.C. went great. Of course, we ended up sleeping together. I knew having her in the house would be too much temptation, but if I put her up in a hotel, she would've been suspicious and assumed it was because of a woman. I definitely didn't want her jumping to *that* conclusion. I had every intention of sleeping on the sofa and letting her have the master suite, but that never happened. Connecting physically came so naturally, and neither of us put up much resistance.

Before the sun even had a chance to set the first day, I laid her across the bed as she was begging me to hurt her real good. I guess all along I knew it would happen, and was looking forward to it. Hell, what can I say? Naomi got a brotha sprung.

Afterwards, I was breathing heavy and hoping to doze off for a minute. But all that loving I'd put down gave Naomi a burst of energy I guess, because she started talking and then expected me to join in on the conversation.

"You may be surprised to know that all this time I've been a little intimidated by the other women in your life."

"Oh, really?" *That ain't no damn news flash,* I thought. "Well, there are no other women in my life now." Naomi's head was in the crook of my arm and I pulled her in, kissed her forehead, and relaxed my head against the pillow.

"No, that's not what I'm talking about. I mean your sisters and your mother."

"What?"

"I never expected them to welcome me the way they did on Sunday. When I dropped Sydney off and Sweetie asked me to stay for dinner to help celebrate her birthday, I was shocked. And they all showed up at D.J.'s game last Friday night. I didn't expect any of that."

"That's how we do sometimes," I explained. "I mentioned I was going to the game and the next thing you know, everybody's tagging along." My eyes were getting heavier by the second. After waiting such a long time and finally getting that warm, wet... well, anyway, I was zapped. "Everybody in my family is cool like that. Well, for the most part."

"Yeah, I know Glory don't like me much…"

"Who? Glo? Oh, yeah. She be trippin' sometime." I yawned. "Baby, I can barely keep my eyes open. Let me get about ten winks. All right?" I turned over. She was still saying something and seconds later, I heard the shower water running.

When I awakened a couple of hours later, Naomi had unpacked all the boxes in my bathrooms, organized my linen closet, and was busy in the kitchen putting dishes away. She made a comment about how she just couldn't understand how I could live like that, with all my things still packed up. For a second, I got angry at the thought of her snooping through my shit, but I was so glad she helped me out, so I let it go. After all, I didn't have anything to hide.

Naomi and I drove over to the school about noon the next day; she was scheduled to speak at one o'clock. The bulk of instruction was done in the morning, leaving afternoons for hands-on learning. Since business was slow on Tuesdays, it was the perfect time to schedule a speaker.

The presentation Naomi put together surprised me. I knew she was an intelligent woman, but I didn't expect her to go all out the way she did. On the drive up, she had the back of my car packed full of stuff she said she would be using, but I didn't ask any questions. Then she spent all morning getting prepared for her lecture. She was so focused she wouldn't even let me get at her one last time, even though she knew it would be our last opportunity for a while.

When speaking to the students, Naomi shared her personal experiences on how she became a salon owner, and gave them all of the pros and cons of being in business for oneself. She had a PowerPoint presentation on time management in the salon and properly booking appointments. I sat at the back of the room, thoroughly impressed. Besides the fact that the skirt she wore was hugging those luscious hips of hers, I couldn't take my eyes off of her. The group seemed to connect with her, too, which surprised me a little. The sight of her in front of a room of eager students showed me a side of Naomi I didn't expect to see: a warm, patient, funny side. I liked what I saw.

Something about that moment changed things for me. Since our break-up, she had been trying so hard to prove that all of the drama was in the past. I could see that she was sincere, that she had really changed. So, on the way to the airport I told her I wanted us to try and work through our problems and give it another try. I made it clear that I wasn't interested in spending a lot of time trying to find out if it was going to work or not because it shouldn't take us long to come to a conclusion. But I also told her that if we *could* make it work for both of us, we should get married and make it official. She looked shocked and before she misunderstood me I made it clear that I was not proposing I just wanted her to know where my head was. I also told her I wasn't gonna tolerate any of her game-playing this time. She agreed, and in true form, she came back with, "And I ain't gon' put up with you fuckin' around on me either." I smiled. I expected nothing less.

Chapter 19 *Glory*

I was just feeling a little something...

All this time I hadn't run into him, seen him from afar, or anything. A couple of times I tried to pull his name into conversations with Dyann, but she didn't catch on. I didn't want her to know I was sweating her cousin anyway, so I stopped dropping hints. RoShon had that thing about him I just couldn't let go of. There were a million reasons why I shouldn't have still been thinking about him and only a few reasons why I should. And those few reasons were right in my face.

I walked into a sandwich shop about ten minutes from Joyce's house to pick up lunch for Frannie, Sweetie, and me. It was well after the lunch rush, so the place was pretty much empty. There he was, all thugged-out, sitting in the corner, sending messages on his two-way. Even though I hadn't seen him in months, I didn't have to question if it was

RoShon. All of my senses that were called to attention let me know exactly who I was looking at.

RoShon hadn't looked up so I didn't know if I should try and get his attention or wait and see if he noticed me first. As he typed away, I checked him out from head to toe. His locs, which had grown a bit, were pulled back in a knot with a few stray ones tucked behind his ear. Both ears held small silver hoops. He wore a basketball jersey the same color as the sky, which was trimmed in white, and since I wasn't up on my teams I didn't know whose it was. Underneath was a crisp white t-shirt that showed off his fit physique. His jeans were baggy and his white sneakers with light-blue trim were untied. Why I found this so appealing, I didn't know. But he exuded so much confidence I couldn't concentrate on what it was I was supposed to be doing.

"May I help you?"

"Ah... yeah." I responded to the young chick who was tapping a finger at the edge of the register.

I stood back from the counter looking over the menu. I couldn't remember what kind of sandwiches I was supposed to be picking up. I think Sweetie wanted tuna or chicken salad and Frannie wanted something so crazy I knew I should've written it down when she said it. Oh damn. "Give me a minute."

I was about to get out my cell and call the shop when I heard his voice. "Glory. Yo—girl, what's up?"

My whole nervous system went into overdrive. The way RoShon said my name was as if the sky had opened up and a chorus of God's best angels began to sing. He almost made me wet myself. I turned around slowly, trying not to look too anxious, but the smile on my face surely let the cat out of the bag.

"RoShon. How are you?"

"I'm cool—I'm cool."

He opened his arms for a hug but I was a little afraid of touching him thinking that I might not want to let go.

"Give me some love, girl."

Oh, Jesus! His body was so solid and he smelled all manly too—like soap and hard work all mixed together.

"I ain't seen you in a minute. Where you been hiding?" he asked, as if we were long-lost friends.

I cleared my throat and tried to pull myself together. "I can't believe you even remember my name."

"Now, how could I forget a name like Glory? And look at you, it fits you so perfectly."

"I saw you when I walked in," I stammered. I didn't really know what to say to RoShon, so I hoped that he would carry the conversation. The girl at the counter walked off and busied herself with something else.

"You wasn't gon' holla?"

"I was waiting on the right moment. You looked busy." RoShon was checking me out from head to toe and I tried to remember what I was looking like. I had dressed down for work, wearing a pair of khaki Bermuda shorts and a turquoise tank top with several silver bangles up my arm. Of course the 'do was done. At that moment I prayed I looked younger.

We conversed for a few moments, reflecting on the night we'd last seen each other. I was so sure this time RoShon was going to ask to see me again, but it never happened. He was wrapping things up, about to say goodbye. I didn't want to go months again waiting to run into him, so I did something I'd never had to do.

"So, what's up, RoShon?"

He was backing up with his hand raised ready to bounce, then stopped. "What's up with what?"

I folded my arms across my chest lifting my breasts. "I know you can tell that I'm feeling you."

He gave a little chuckle.

"Really, what's up? I've been waiting on you to ask to see me again, or my phone number, something. I know you young brothas are used to women hounding you but I'm old school. I'm used to being approached *and* pursued."

"Is that right?" He had an amused look on his face. "Approaching a woman ain't a problem for me; I just never would've guessed you'd be checking for a brotha like me."

"Why, because of the age difference?"

"Naw, not really that, but look at you. All prim, proper, and preppy. I'm straight up hood and I make no apologies for it."

"So, you not checking for me?" I was using his words, trying to show that I was down.

"No doubt, the chemistry is there. But it takes more than that for me. You're beautiful, sexy, and I can tell you got conversation. And back in the day that would've been enough. Now, any woman I'm checking for has to have a personal relationship with Christ."

Did he just say Christ—as in Jesus?

"I go to church," I blurted out.

"That's not what I said."

"So, what, you think you're better than me?"

"I'm sorry. I didn't mean to come off like that. I'm just struggling to stay on the straight and narrow. And trust—back in the day, by now you would already be my ex and we'd both be on to the next."

Was that supposed to be a compliment?

"Don't get me confused with some chicken head." I needed to regain my composure. "I ain't looking for someone to carry me if that's what you were thinking. *I got that.* I was just feeling a little something—it's not that serious."

"Hold up. Don't get all twisted on me. For real, I ain't that nigga no more. Hit and quit it. I'm trying to be about something different." He pulled his two-way out of his pocket. "You know what? Let me get your number so we can talk."

"Don't do me any favors." I turned toward the counter looking for ol' girl.

"Hold on." RoShon touched my arm. "I'm sorry. I didn't mean it like that. I would *really* like to have them digits."

"No. Really, it's okay. It was nice seeing you again."

Chick walked up and I started making up an order. "Let me get a tuna on wheat, a six-inch meatball sandwich on white and, let's see... what do I want? Just give me the special, whatever that is."

Without turning around I heard RoShon walk out of the glass doors. I felt embarrassed, to say the least, that I let this young Negro get at me the way I had. After regaining the small amount of dignity I had splattered onto the floor, Chick walked up with all of my food bagged up. I had no idea what was in the sacks, but figured Frannie and Sweetie would make do with whatever it was.

I walked to my car and found a business card slid between the glass and the rubber of the driver's side window. I took the card out. It belonged to RoShon Richardson, and suggested that he was the owner of a janitorial service. On the back he had written his home number down and two words. PLEASE CALL.

"Tha hell!"

~~~

I could hear Frannie getting started in the back room and I just ignored her. She'd been acting foul all week.

"Glo! What is this shit?"

I could hear Sweetie too. "This looks like tuna— I thought I asked for chicken salad."

"Glo!"

"Oh well, this don't taste bad." Sweetie was so easy to please.

"I'm not eating this. And I ain't paying for it either."

"The hell you ain't." I walked in on them complaining.

"The hell I *am*! You do this shit on purpose so won't nobody ask you to go pick up lunch. You ain't slick."

"What's the problem? I thought you asked for a meatball sandwich."

"You *know* I ain't asked for a damn meatball sandwich. Does that even sound like some shit I would ask for?"

"Actually, it does." I sucked my teeth, "Girl, you better eat that *and* give me my money."

I walked out. I had been gone so long trippin' off RoShon that my next client was already pulling into the drive. I had missed my opportunity to enjoy my lunch while it was fresh.

"Just eat mine and shut the hell up," I called out from up front. Sweetie was busy eating, but I could still hear Frannie talking crazy. I didn't care. I had lost my appetite anyway thinking about what had happened at the deli. Hopefully work would get my mind off it.

Chapter 20 *Frannie*

I knew she would let me in.

"You should go back to the doctor," Michael said, sliding under the covers next to me. He placed his hand on my hip. "I don't think it's normal that you've been feeling tired for so long."

I nestled in closer to my pillow.

"What do you think?"

"You're probably right," I said. "But I think it'll pass."

"Are you still taking your vitamins everyday?"

"Umm... yeah."

"It's been several weeks. You should be feeling better by now."

"Um-hmm." I wanted Michael to stop touching me. I didn't want him to mess around, get an erection, and end up going to sleep frustrated.

He reached for the remote and turned on the TV. "Make yourself an appointment tomorrow."

"All right," I said, closing my eyes.

~~~

I'd been knocking on Joyce's front door and ringing the bell for some time. I peeked through the window and could see her finally coming to let me in. When she opened the door I couldn't believe how young she looked. Her hair was jet black.

"Hi, can I help you?" she said, sweetly.

"Can you help me?"

I could see Wendell, Glory, and Sweetie sitting around the table. They were all laughing and eating. Grandma Francine walked out of the kitchen holding a casserole dish, and I could smell a pot roast and homemade dinner rolls.

"Are you looking for the Jackson's? They live next door." Joyce pointed in the direction of our long-time neighbor's home.

"Joyce, stop playing. Are you mad that I'm late?" I approached the entryway and she slammed the door in my face. What kind of game were they playing? I stood there for a few minutes, waiting on her to re-open the door and say she was just teasing, even though Joyce didn't usually joke around like that. I didn't know what to think.

I waited and waited and nothing. I walked back to the window and saw they were all still sitting at the table eating like it was any other day. I wondered where Michael and the kids were. His truck wasn't in the driveway. I wanted to see if he had parked in the back.

As I walked, little white rocks kept sticking to the bottoms of my shoes. In between steps I tried shaking the pebbles loose. I became so frustrated that I ran back to the front porch to get away from the gravel.

I knocked on the window trying to get Sweetie's attention. I knew she would let me in.

"Sweetie, open the door! What are y'all doing?"

They all went along with dinner as though they didn't hear me. Joyce and Wendell were sitting at either end of the table. Sweetie and Glory sat on one side, and Grandma Francine and Michael sat on the other.

"Michael let me in! This ain't funny."

All of a sudden Joyce went from sitting at the table to standing right in front of the window with her face pressed to the glass. It frightened me so much that I jumped back. She was yelling and screaming and cursing me out with the ugliest look on her face. As she screamed, foam flew from her mouth and splattered on the window.

I shot straight up in bed with sweat beaded up on my forehead.

Michael sat up next to me and rubbed my back. I was breathing hard and trying to shake off the effects of the nasty vision of Joyce in the window.

"What's the matter?" he asked, with sleepy concern. "You've been tossing and turning."

My mouth was dry and I couldn't speak.

"You sick?" He turned on the lamp.

I was burning up so I threw back the covers.

"Baby, looks like you finally started your period." The word *finally* hung in the air for a moment. So, he *had* noticed that I hadn't gotten it. A familiar feeling of suffocation came over me.

"I was starting to get excited thinking you might be pregnant again," he said. We both got out of the bed.

I had obviously bled through my pad. The doctor at the clinic said the bleeding would be heavy the first couple of days.

Chapter 21 Joyce

It was total reverberation.

"Good morning, Miss Joyce."

"Good morning, Rob. You need me to sign for something?" Rob didn't do his usual of sticking the mail in the box and waving from the curb.

"Yeah. Looks like an important letter. Return receipt." He handed me a pen and placed his finger where he wanted me to sign.

"Um. Okay." I was sitting on the porch enjoying the morning when our postman of ten years walked up palming a stack of envelopes and sales ads.

It was the kind of morning that made me feel at peace, like everything was all right in the world. I had been sipping decaf, eating yogurt with granola mixed in and enjoying the welcomed season change of mild weather.

When I got an adequate look at the letter there was a little shift in my countenance. I wasn't expecting anything but then again letters like this were always unexpected. Coming from the law offices of Wolinsky, somebody and somebody... I set the letter aside and took a long sip of my coffee, which was beginning to cool. I started on the other mail first: a $49 water bill; an application for a platinum Master Card; a thank you note for a wedding gift from a ceremony I'd attended four months ago; and a bill for my *O Magazine* subscription, then finally the letter. I said a quick prayer before flipping it over and lifting the seal.

> *Dear Joyce Parker,*
>
> *We are contacting you on behalf of Josephine Doherty, a.k.a. Josephine Espinoza, in reference to the trust of the deceased, Doctor Carlos Espinoza. This notice is in the matter of the son/daughter born of Respondent, Joyce Parker and the deceased.*
>
> *We are requesting your appearance on Tuesday, March 6, at 10:00 A.M. at the Law Offices of Wolinsky, Imperioli, Merth, and Krane, located at 909 E. 1st Street, Wichita, Kansas 67212. If you are unable to keep this appointment please call to reschedule. Nothing is required of you except your appearance. All questions or inquiries will be addressed at the meeting time.*
>
> *Thank you kindly,*
> *Anthony Imperioli, Esq.*

The thumping of a drum was in my head. I could feel the vibration beating through my skin and inside my chest. Sound waves appeared on the surface of my coffee; it was total reverberation. I looked up and there was a bright yellow, '67 Chevy moving down the street with its music shaking up the neighborhood. My heart seemed to be synchronized with the fading base of the music from the passing car.

I read the letter again. *Josephine Espinoza.* I never dreamed I would hear her name again, let alone have her contact me. What could this be about? Doherty was the name she was going by now. Did she remarry? Was that her maiden name? The word *trust* was used. What did that mean? I couldn't imagine that Carlos would have left Sweetie any money—she hadn't even been born at the time of his accident. And if there was money, why was it just now coming up? *All questions would be answered at the meeting.* The suspense would surely kill me before then.

I read the letter for a third time. It wasn't chock full of information, to say the least, but there had to be some clues somewhere. Was this correspondence friendly or hostile? The attorney said I didn't need to bring anything to the meeting, but I wouldn't fall for that. After giving it more thought, I came up with some things to be sure I had with me. Sweetie's birth certificate, pictures of Carlos and me... what else might I need?

Oh God! Would Josephine be there? Would I finally get to see what she looked like after all these years? And she would finally see me. Or maybe she already had.

My mind was going in a million different directions, making the whole thing more monstrous than it probably was. I stopped, took a deep breath, and leaned back in my chair.

"Mama! You didn't hear the phone ringing?" Sweetie burst through the front door nearly giving me a heart attack. I turned the letter over and grabbed my chest.

"Girl! You scared me half to death. What's wrong with you?"

"Oh, I'm sorry. I've been calling you from the shop. I saw your car still in the garage and couldn't figure out why you weren't answering the phone."

"I don't always hear it when I'm out here on the porch."

"Oh." Sweetie looked down at my lap. "Miss Betty wants to know if you can do her hair today. She's got a wake to attend this evening."

"Tell her yes. Anytime after one." I gathered up the mail and walked past her through the front door.

I wanted to tell her about the letter I'd received, but needed more time to process things. I honestly couldn't remember how much I had already told her about Carlos. She didn't know her father was married to another woman and had two other small children when she was conceived. Even though she loved me and knew I wasn't perfect, I didn't want to disappoint her by giving all of the sordid details.

What would Sweetie think? Would it be best if I went to the meeting alone, to find out what this was all about before involving her? It was all too much to think about.

Chapter 22 *Sweetie*

He loved you even without knowing you...

Shacking up was something none of us had ever done. But here I was, trying to decide if I should let Ric move in. He had been dropping hints for weeks—at least what I called hints. He'd been taking care of the lawn, cleaning out the garage. He'd even hired someone to clear out the gutters. The pipe in the sprinkler system was leaking water into the basement so he took care of that, too.

I knew he was having a money situation, but it would've killed him to come out and ask to move in. If things had been reversed, he wouldn't have hesitated to help me out so the decision was an easy one. I decided to let him take up residence with me. The trick would be to do it in a way that wouldn't leave him feeling less than a man. I had to make him believe that I needed him to move in more than he needed to move in.

Before my birthday dinner at Mama's house, Ric was sulking. I didn't really know what was wrong with him, but I'd learned not to ask. My actual birthday was the previous Friday, and he had taken me to dinner and given me a beautiful pair of diamond earrings. I loved my present, but I got the feeling he didn't think it was enough. To make him feel better, I made this little speech telling him how happy I was with him; happier than I'd been in a long time. I let him know, that him being in my life was the best gift he could've ever given me. He might as well have been on another planet. He didn't hear a word I said.

At Mama's, everyone admired my earrings and was more than cordial to Ric, even Wendell. I'm sure they couldn't tell anything was wrong with him, but I could. I knew he didn't think his gift was elaborate enough, even though it was. I was completely satisfied, but he accused me of being disappointed. And me going on and on about how much I loved them, just seemed to make it worse.

~~~

"Sweetie, I got a letter the other day." Mama's voice was barely coming through the rush of water hitting the porcelain sink.

"Yeah, she's been acting strange lately," I said, thinking about Frannie's odd behavior. Her attitude all week had been bothering me. Once I even caught her crying in the back room. I asked her what was wrong; she told me to, "*Mind my own damn business.*" Those were words I would've expected from Glory but not from her. I thought surely she was going to come back later and apologize, but she never did.

Mama was shampooing my hair, our weekly ritual. I loved the way she massaged my scalp, it was so relaxing and it also gave us some time together.

"We need to go... me and you, we have an appointment—"

"Huh?" I asked, confused.

Mama turned off the water and stood looking at me. She was wearing the smock she wore when she painted, and there were dried paint stains down the front. I could hear Bryce and Kevin in the other room arguing over what to watch on television while they waited on me.

"Can you not hear me?" Mama looked at me quizzically.

"I heard you. You're talking about Frannie?"

"No. I said you and I have an appointment we need to keep on Tuesday."

"What kind of an appointment?"

Mama pumped shampoo into her hand then applied it to my hair. She worked it until she got a thick lather going, and then spoke.

"I got a letter the other day. I'm not exactly sure what it means, but it's from a relative of your father's."

I didn't know what to say so I waited for her to go on.

"The meeting is at an attorney's office, down-town."

"Who is the relative?" I asked.

"The attorney contacted me on behalf of Carlos' wife. I'm not sure what it all means, but you were mentioned. And, something about a trust."

"Oh." I wanted to ask her what she meant by *his wife* but didn't. I could tell she felt uneasy talking to me about it. "You think he left some money for me?"

"I can't see how. I told you he died before you were even born. He didn't even know if you were a boy or a girl. His... um... his wife knew about you, but she never contacted me after he was killed. And, of course... I um, never contacted her either."

"Oh."

Mama turned the water on and rinsed my hair. We were silent. I wanted to know more, but didn't want to make her any more uncomfortable than she already was.

"What time are we supposed to be there?"

She turned off the water again and stood motionless. "Ten. They only requested my presence, but I thought you should come because it's obviously about you. You are the only link I have to Carlos."

Mama began tearing up. I could see she still loved him very much and my heart ached for her. She'd only spoken of him a few times and it was always emotional for her.

I closed my eyes and took a deep breath. "It's okay, Mama."

"I want you to come, but only if you want to."

"Of course, I'll go."

"I want you to know..." the tears were coming now. "You should know that he was very excited about you coming. He loved you even without knowing you... he loved me, too."

~~~

When I pulled into my driveway I could see that Ric had been working in the yard. The two large, blue spruce trees in front had been perfectly trimmed and pruned. The yard had been cut and edged, and not one loose blade was to be found on the cement, unlike when I did the lawn myself. Garbage bags full of mowed grass and loose brush were stacked neatly against the dumpster at the curb.

The boys and I entered the house and found it was spotless. I went up the stairs to my bedroom. The room was clean and a stint of shower steam still hung in the air in the bathroom, but no Ric. He hadn't left a note so I had no idea if he planned on coming back that evening.

"Bryce and Kevin! Somebody go take a bath. I don't care who goes first," I yelled, as I walked back towards their room.

I heard them arguing, trying to make the other go first, but nobody moved toward the bathroom.

"You want me to pick who goes?"

"Yeah, Mama. You pick." I knew Bryce would speak up first.

"Okay. Then you go, Bryce." I stood in the doorway of their bedroom. "And Kevin, you clean this mess while he's in the tub."

"Aw, Mama!" they both said together.

"Is Ric coming back over tonight?" Kevin asked.

"Yeah," Bryce said. "Can we wait up for him? It's Friday."

"I don't know. Do what I asked you both to do and we'll see."

I showered, flat ironed my hair, and got ready for bed. It was after eleven and I figured I would stay up with the boys a while before turning in, maybe watch a movie. But when I went to see if they wanted to join me, they were both asleep on the floor in front of the PlayStation. When I looked in their bathroom and saw the mess they'd left, I started to wake them up, but they were sleeping so peacefully. Instead, I straightened up, turned off their television, and put them both to bed.

I went down to the den and put in a movie, but nodded off before the opening credits finished. I was woken up a few hours later when I heard Ric at the door.

I rubbed my eyes and glanced at the clock. It was two in the morning. "Oh hey, baby."

Ric didn't say anything. I laid back down, fully expecting him to come over and kiss me hello. When he didn't, I lifted my head again and took a closer look. His lower lip was bleeding and I could tell he was worked up. I jumped up from the couch and went to him.

"You're bleeding. What happened?"

"Where?" He touched his face.

"Your mouth!" I noticed the abrasions on the back of his hand. "Have you been fighting?"

He looked at the back of his hand and walked away from me. "I just got beat out of a shit load of money," he mumbled.

"What! You were gambling?"

Ric gave me a strange look. "Yeah. You could say that." Upon closer inspection I could see that his

Polo button-down was ripped at the shoulder, and there was dirt on the knees of his slacks.

"Are you okay?" I was afraid for him and for me. I didn't know what was happening. "Should I be afraid for you?"

He continued to walk back and forth next to the dining room table. His mind was a million miles away.

"Should I be afraid for all of us? Is someone after you?" I watched as he continued to walk back and forth across the floor. "Ric, what's going on—say something."

Ric looked at me for a long while, then turned and walked out the door. I was up the whole night calling his cell and worrying that something terrible had happened to him.

The next morning, bloodshot eyes, complete with bags underneath them to match, I dragged myself, along with the boys, out of the house. I dropped them off at Frannie and Michael's and made my way to the salon. I was thankful for the short day, but seriously considered canceling all my appointments. How could I concentrate on work when I was worried sick about Ric?

Chapter 23 Wendell

... the very thing I said I'd never do.

"What do you think everybody's gonna say?"

"Um... em," was my answer. I reached over and ran my fingers through Naomi's hair. I had the top down on the Jag and her curls were blowing freely in the wind.

"My mother is gonna be pissed at first, but hopefully she'll think of all the time and money that was saved and get over it," Naomi said, leaning her head into my hand.

She clutched the bouquet of flowers in her lap as loose petals slid from her lap to the floor. "I should've said something," she continued. "We both should have."

"Yeah. You're probably right."

"How do you think commuting is gonna work for us?"

"We'll work it out," I assured her.

"Will you come to Wi—"

I put a finger to her lips, cutting her off. "Let's just enjoy these next few days. We'll worry about everything else when we get back." I pulled her face to mine, meeting her halfway as we raced up I-435. As we kissed, the heat between us was ignited.

Naomi unbuckled her seatbelt and began giving my neck little bites while undoing the belt on my slacks. She reached inside my trousers and I grabbed her hand.

"Are you trying to kill us?" I laughed a little. "Woman, I can't drive while you go down on me."

"Why not? You can't do two things at once?"

"Not those two things. We'll be upside-down in a ditch somewhere."

"Um. Okay. Cuz ain't nothing sexy about crashing." She re-did my buckle and sat back in her seat.

"I'd pull over if we weren't trying to catch a flight."

"I dare you."

I laughed. "Have I told you how beautiful you look today?"

"Yes. You have."

Naomi and I made plans to get married before either of us had time to talk ourselves out of it. No pre-marital counseling, no engagement; we hadn't even cleared away all the debris from the past. We were jumping headfirst into it, the very thing I said I'd never do.

We applied for a marriage license two weeks before and decided that when it arrived, we would just do it. And that's what we did. No one but the two of us knew our plans. We both agreed that keeping it to ourselves would be for the best. We headed off to Scottsdale, Arizona for a honeymoon spa retreat. Our plan was to tell everybody when we returned.

The first full day at New Beginnings Spa Retreat, we had been sharing a mud bath for half an hour and drinking Champaign when I asked Naomi a question that I had been asking myself. The bath was heated and soothing and we had just enjoyed his and hers full body massages so our minds were clear.

"Baby, how do you really feel about us getting married the way we did?"

With a terry cloth turban wrapped around her head, Naomi leaned back on the edge of the marble tub. "Excited." She lifted her head and looked at me. "What about you?"

I pondered my answer to the question.

"Come on." I stood, took Naomi by the hand, and helped her out. We walked over to the shower built for two, leaving a trail of warm wet dirt. Temperate water sprayed on us from four showerheads. We rubbed each other's bodies as the muck rinsed away and washed down the drain. She clung to me in the same way the mud had only moments earlier. We kissed and made good use of the oversized shower room.

"I finally got my woman."

"Yes, you do."

"I love you."

"Yes… you do."

...I wasn't in the mood for intrusions

THA HELL! Joyce asked me to stop by Crandall's Bakery for her. She said she was—actually, she said *we* were putting a reception together. Something about Wendell and Naomi returning from their honeymoon.

"I'll need you to get it by three tomorrow—" there was a break in her words indicating another call coming in on her end. "Hold on." She clicked over.

Bump that! I sat there holding the phone in amazement half a second before I hung up. I couldn't believe it. Wendell married that girl! I wouldn't be picking up a wedding cake *or* going to that damn reception. As much as I loved Sydney, I hated her mother double that. Alright, maybe hate was a strong word. If Wendell hadn't married her, I could've tolerated her, but Naomi being in the Parker family was making me feel sick.

I dialed Wendell's mobile number. It rang once before I hung up. What would I say to him? Ask him if he was crazy? Cuss him out for being so stupid? No, I couldn't do either of those things. But I could certainly let them all know how I felt about it through my absence.

The next day, hours before the reception, Frannie called me four times trying to confirm that I was picking up the cake. I didn't answer or call her back. I'd let them figure it out.

My phone had been ringing all day. Not just Joyce and Frannie, but other family and friends calling me about the reception in general. I didn't answer anybody's call. Forget them—including Wendell and Naomi.

At the time the party would've been getting underway, my freshly showered, lightly perfumed and moisturized body was lying on top of my caramel-colored duvet. Gazing up at the stone-colored sheers draped around the canopy that came just short of the ceiling, I spotted a couple of spider webs. I considered getting up there to clear them away, but decided it wasn't the kind of mood I was in.

I pulled open the drawer to my nightstand where I had put RoShon's business card. I had taken it out and looked it over many times, so with automation I grabbed it, gazed over his name a few times, then flipped it and read the plea from him on the back. PLEASE CALL.

Not only would it be a nice diversion from the situation with Wendell, but I realized I was ready to finally connect with RoShon. I picked up the phone, took a deep breath, and then dialed the number.

"This Rich!" The voice was loud and raspy. I wondered if maybe I'd misdialed.

"Um, hello. I'm trying to reach RoShon Richardson."

"Yeah. This is RoShon Richardson," he said, a little more calmly.

"Oh, hey. This is Glory."

"Yo, Ma! What's up?" He sounded happy to hear from me.

"Nothin' much." I was hoping the relief I felt didn't come through. I didn't want him to know how nervous I was.

"I was beginning to think I'd never hear from you." He was moving about, slightly out of breath.

"I never expected to call you."

"Oh. So, is this a business call?"

"Oh, no. It's personal." I put some sexy on that.

"You know how to make a brotha sweat, don't you?" He was starting to settle down.

"What do you mean?" I lay on my back with my legs in the air, examining my fresh pedicure.

"I really wanted a chance to make that thang right. You know, from the last time I saw you."

"Oh, really?"

"I thought you'd never call and just go on hating on a brotha."

"I'm surprised you even gave it a second thought the way you were blowing me off."

"Can we get together and talk?"

"Sure."

"What you doin' later? Maybe we could meet for coffee or if you haven't eaten yet…"

"Are you asking me out after I had to degrade myself and ask why you wasn't trying to get with me?"

RoShon laughed. "A brotha *tryin'* to make it up to you. Besides, I want to see you again."

I smiled. That was exactly what I wanted to hear. "All right. I'm free."

"What you feel like?"

What I felt like was his large, hard body on top of mine, diverting my attention from all of this reception mess. But since that wouldn't be happening... "I could go for a good hamburger."

"Okay." I heard a little hesitation. "How about that bar and grill across the street from the sandwich shop I saw you at last time?"

"I'll meet you there in an hour."

"Can't wait." He disconnected the call.

With a burst of new energy I jumped off the bed and dashed to the closet. I had hundreds upon hundreds of articles of clothing and wanted to choose carefully. I wanted to be myself, but careful not to wear something that would make me look too old.

For forty-five minutes I tossed around blouses, slacks, dresses, and blue jeans. A short skirt would be too revealing for the religious side of him, and a hem too far below the knee might make me look my age, which was something I didn't want to do. Jeans were an option, but seemed so typical. If they were tight they would get his attention, but I didn't want to come off as cheap either.

RoShon really had me going. I wanted to be mad at him, but I was mad at myself. The whole thing was driving me bananas. I had wasted forty-five minutes trying to decide what to wear and had fifteen minutes to get to the spot. At the height of my frustration I decided to just be myself and threw on a long white skirt and a fitted white t-shirt with rhinestone-studded trim. Taking a final look at myself in the mirror, I decided I didn't give a damn what he thought. By the time I got there, fifteen minutes late, I started giving a damn once again.

Why was I tripping like this? Was it because he didn't start out sweating me like every other man that I came across? Or was there just something about him? I pondered that thought for a moment. There *was* something about him. He had that thing—that thing that just did it for me.

"Hi RoShon. Sorry, I'm late," I said as I walked up. When I arrived at the restaurant, he was sitting at the bar talking with the bartender. "I guess I needed a little more than an hour."

RoShon stood, giving me a hug that made me want to melt. It was so encompassing, heartfelt and genuine.

"Yo, Ma. I'd have waited all night," he said, through glistening white teeth.

I tugged at the collar of his pin striped, over-sized, button down shirt. "Oh, so there it is."

"Yo, what's that?"

"The charm that I didn't think you had."

RoShon laughed. "Before the evening is over, the image you have of me is gonna change." The peach and white of his shirt complemented his Hershey complexion perfectly.

"I hope you're right."

He smiled confidently. "Come on. Let's see if our table is ready." He placed his hand gently at the small of my back and every nerve ending in my body tingled.

The hostess seated us in a secluded area of the restaurant. Under any other circumstances I would've been offended that we were being stuck in the back, but being with RoShon made it romantic. Double's Bar & Grill had a cool, industrial-type atmosphere. It wasn't cozy per se, but thanks to present company, my insides were warming up. The floor was a shellacked concrete and the walls were brown and dark orange. The warm feeling I got being with him removed the chill from the contrasting décor.

"They have some of the best burgers here. Have you ever had one?" I didn't need to look over the menu. I knew exactly what I would be getting.

"No, I haven't." His eyes were so bright and clear, as if he'd never seen a day of stress or worry.

"You'll love 'em."

"I'm a vegetarian. A vegan, actually."

I raised an eyebrow. "A vegan?"

"Yeah, I don't eat anything that comes from an animal."

"I *know* what a vegan is."

"Oh, my bad. But, you get yo' eat on. Don't let that stop you."

"Don't worry, I won't."

RoShon laughed as if he had an inside joke and I ignored it. I wanted to order a drink to calm my nerves, but the server hadn't made it to our table yet.

I leaned back to get a good look under the table at homeboy's footwear. "Those better be vinyl," I said, "since you're so worried about the cow."

He laughed again. "I don't eat it; I didn't say I couldn't wear it."

"One thing I can't stand is a hypocrite."

RoShon laughed, but ignored my challenge.

We looked at each other for a moment. He held my gaze with a pleased expression. I appreciated his stare because it gave me the opportunity to get a good look at him, too.

"You look like an angel in all that white, Ma."

I blushed. "Thank you."

"You a beautiful sistah." He was nodding his head slowly in approval.

"You almost sound intimidated."

"I probably am, a little. I don't mind admitting it."

"I can't imagine you thinking I'm too much for you."

He did that laugh again. It was getting on my nerves because I didn't know what it meant.

"Okay, what's with the little chuckle?"

"Nuttin', Ma. You just make a brotha wanna backslide."

"Is that a compliment?"

"Definitely. Back in the day, I would've been trying to go home with you the night we met. You that fine."

"Oh really?"

"True story." His expression switched up and turned timid. He picked up his glass to finish off the rest of his Pepsi and regained his composure. "But that's the old me. Degrading women and making them think they have to be hos in order to have a man's attention."

Our server interrupted to tell us about the specials and take our orders. RoShon ordered vegetable soup to start and a veggie burger that had all the appeal of charcoal-broiled cardboard between two slices of wet paper. He asked for a baked potato instead of French-fries, and I wondered, if he didn't eat butter, sour cream, or cheese, what did he put on it? With anybody else, this shit would've gotten on my nerves for real, but I was chilling. He appealed to me that much.

I ordered my hamburger, complete with a big ol' side of fries. Then I asked the server to bring me a Corona. I needed to loosen up.

"What did you mean by that?" I asked, after the waiter departed.

"By what?"

"About a man making a woman a ho... What were you saying?"

"Men do it all the time. Make a woman think she wants to sex them, when what she really wants is a relationship. She screws him thinking she's going to get what she wants in the end, but most likely gets left when something better comes along. I was one of those men who turned women into hos."

"That's an arrogant way of looking at it, thinking you possess that kind of power over women. Some women actually choose to sleep around."

"A woman can never turn herself into a ho. Only a man can do that," RoShon said.

"I don't think so."

"True story."

"Actually, I'm of the small minority of people who believe *all* women are hos on some level." I thrive on shock value, but I actually meant what I was saying. I waited on his reaction.

"What?" He was startled, as I knew he would be.

"It's true. Women just don't want to admit it because the term and the actual profession carry such a negative stigma."

"That's an interesting position coming from a woman. How do you figure?"

I sat back in my seat. "What's your definition of a ho? Give it to me."

"A person, male or female," he emphasized, "that has sex or performs some sexual act in exchange for something, usually something of monetary value."

"Okay." I allowed him to settle into the pleasure of his definition. "And would you agree that most people believe that to be the definition?"

He hunched his shoulders. "Yeah, I guess."

"Well, if that's true, then all sexually active women, especially married women, are hos. Every woman uses sex as a bargaining tool, I don't care who she is. If a woman wants something from her husband, what does she do? She gives him good sex."

RoShon was laughing, but at the same time, hanging on my every word. Finally, he said, "You make a valid point. Although, I don't know if I totally agree with it."

"It's innate in the female psyche. We rarely ever give up sex without getting something in return; at least not a smart woman. Give it some thought."

"I'll do that."

The server brought his soup and my drink. RoShon extended his hands across the table, beckoning me to take hold, which I did. He bowed his head and asked God to bless our meal. I wondered if the prayer included my frosty bottle of beer.

When he finished, he picked up his spoon and stirred the vegetables around several times. "I'm really glad you called me."

"So am I." I took a swig. If Joyce could see me she'd cringe at the fact that I hadn't asked for a glass.

"Can I ask you a question?" he asked, tasting his soup.

"Sure."

"I've never seen so much hair on one person. I can't be the first person to ask..."

"Yes, it's all mine, if that's what you were wondering."

"Just curious. I hope I didn't offend you."

"No. But since we're asking questions, I have one."

"What's up, Ma? What you want to know?" He continued with his soup.

"You don't eat meat, you don't drink, and you don't sleep around. What are your vices?"

"My diet is a result of the high blood pressure and heart disease that runs rampant in my family. I don't drink because I have an estranged brother that's done enough drugs and drinking for all of us, so I guess you could say I never acquired a taste for it. The sex thing, well, I'm still struggling with that one, on the real.

"Yo, I'm not trying to put myself out there like I don't do anything wrong. I can be just as crooked as the next person if I don't check myself. I just want to live more righteous. Be a better man."

"That's commendable and all, but I don't think there's anything wrong with a few faults in a person."

"Trust me, I have faults. If God blesses me to be in your life any length of time, you'll get a chance to see them for yourself."

That was the most promising thing RoShon had said thus far. It was nice to have confirmation that he *was* feeling me and we might get a chance to hang out more.

"Hey, Glo." Juanita, an old neighbor who grew up down the street from us, approached the table. She was wearing a snug, stretchy t-shirt that made her midsection look like biscuits popping out of a can and heels that made an awful clinking sound with every step against the slick cement. "How's it going, girl?"

"Hi, Nita. Haven't seen you in a minute." RoShon and I were finally starting to vibe and I wasn't in the mood for intrusions.

"What are you doing here?" she asked me. RoShon looked up at her. We both found her question a bit odd.

"Just having dinner with a friend." I didn't really want to do introductions, but I also didn't want RoShon to think anything was up. "RoShon, this is Juanita, a friend of the family. Juanita—RoShon."

"What's up?" RoShon was cordial.

"Nice to meet you," she replied, and then turned back to me. "No, I was wondering why you're not at the reception for Wendell?"

"Oh." I had forgotten all about that fiasco and didn't appreciate her reminding me.

"It *is* today, right?" she asked.

"Yeah. It's today." I didn't owe her an explanation and wasn't about to give her one. There was a slight awkwardness I didn't try to smooth out and a silence I didn't try and fill.

"Well, girl. It was cool seeing you. Take care." She walked off, giving me a little wave. The moment was a bit awkward, but I was prepared to go on as if nothing had happened. I placed a napkin in my lap because I could see the server coming with our order.

"So, who's Wendell?"

"My brother."

"Oh, your *brother* got married."

"Yeah," I said, as our food was placed in front of us.

Once the server left, he picked up right where we left off. "Is it safe to ask why you're not at the reception?"

"Hmm? Oh. Just didn't want to go." I lifted my bun and made sure there were no foreign objects lying beneath. Put the tomato on and a little lettuce, but forewent the onion in case RoShon and I touched lips later.

"You're not close? You didn't grow up together?"

"No. We grew up in the same home. And we're very close."

"But you're not showing up to his reception?"

I folded my arms across my chest, feeling defensive. "Are you getting ready to judge me again?"

"No. Don't be so quick to rate my questions. I was just trying to understand. I grew up without my parents and siblings so I don't take for granted the importance of family the way people do that have their family around all of the time."

That may have been a cue for me to ask him about his family but I got the feeling that it was just going to make me feel worse about not going to be with my own family. So I opted to change the subject.

Chapter 25 *Frannie*

I wasn't about to let her disrespect me with her sour mood.

I know it was supposed to be a small reception pulled together at the last minute, but if I was going to do something, I had to do it right. It took a little work, but I found a rental place that carried everything we needed—one-stop shopping. There were two tents draped with white sheers in each corner of the yard. One was to house the three-tier, strawberry chantilly wedding cake, and the other for an inviting gift table complete with a money tree. Parties To Go Rental Company positioned a dance floor of teakwood parquet sections in the middle of the yard, surrounded by small round tables covered with white tablecloths. Each table was topped with a small crystal bowl with lavender gladiola blooms floating in water. The chairs were covered in foam-green or pale, lavender slips, with the opposite color sashes tied around the backs.

The disc jockey, our cousin Butch, was positioned on the patio with amplifiers, speakers, and a light show set up, ready to annoy the neighbors for hours. Joyce and Aunt Jeanette were in the kitchen putting together trays of food, while Michael worked the meat-slicing machine. The boys were upstairs with Michael's mother, getting dressed, while Ericka slept peacefully in her crib.

I was rushing toward a ringing telephone when I heard my name being called.

"Francine, Brandon doesn't have any dress shoes." My mother-in-law was standing at the top of the stairs.

Crandall's Bakery was on the caller ID, which gave me pause. Joyce peeked through the kitchen door. She knew of the mounting tension between Mrs. Thomas and me.

"Yes, he does. He has a brand new pair he just got last week." The cordless phone continued to ring in my hand.

"Well, where are they?" Her voice was growing sharper.

"They're still in the box, on the floor in the boys' closet."

"If you're talking about the brown ones that look like they've never been to church, they don't fit."

The ringing was becoming more insistent and so was Mrs. Thomas.

"Answer that phone," Joyce said to me. She began making her way up the stairs.

Ready to defend me against the enemy, Joyce took over with Mrs. Thomas. "*I* bought those shoes for Brandon last Saturday. *And* they fit him just fine then."

The uninterrupted hum from the meat-slicer, as Michael worked on, pissed me off. I know he heard his mother trying to get some mess started, but I could always count on him to ignore conflict between us two women. As I connected the call I heard Mrs. Thomas's voice soften as she leaned over the banister and saw Joyce on her way up. I wanted to know what was going on upstairs so I was half paying attention until I heard a young woman say the wedding cake had yet to be picked up and they were closing in fifteen minutes.

THAT HEIFA! I *told* Sweetie Glory was tripping. Damn. She could've at least told us she wasn't going to pick up the cake.

"Ma'am, someone will be right over to pick it up if you don't mind waiting, unless you deliver... You do! Great! The address should be on the order."

I didn't have time to give Glory any energy so I decided to save it all up to cuss her out later. Confident that Joyce had handled the situation upstairs, I went to my bedroom to get dressed.

Out of the window I saw people starting to arrive, and Michael filled in as host in my absence. He really knew how to play the role of the perfect spouse when everybody was looking, which really got under my skin at times. He glanced over toward the bedroom, and as we made eye contact he blew me a quick kiss. I thought about responding by giving him the finger, but didn't.

I moved back to the closet, removed a lavender dress from its hanger, and put it on while standing in front of the mirror. As I fluffed my hair, I took a good look at myself for a few minutes. I didn't like what I saw but I was stuck with it. I sucked in my stomach, then exhaled. I had a girdle, but Lord only knew where it was and I didn't have time to look for it. The sleeveless shift showed the excess of my arms but I didn't have time to make another selection. It was the only thing I owned that went well with the color scheme.

"Hey, baby." Michael stepped through door. "Wendell and Naomi are on their way and several people are..."

I stepped away from the mirror and picked up a bottle of perfume.

"...Wow, Francine. You look beautiful." Michael stepped up behind me, put his hands on my shoulders, and gently ran them down my arms. "What's the matter?" he asked, noticing my mood.

"Did you finish slicing the ham and roast beef?"

"Of course." He began kissing my shoulder. "Your mother is putting the food out right now."

Michael turned me around and was coming in for a kiss when the doorbell rang. I broke from his embrace and headed out of the bedroom.

"I think the cake is here. Can you dress Ericka? Her clothes are lying out."

The backyard was full of well-wishers when Wendell and Naomi arrived. The couple was wearing beiges and golds, and it dawned on me that I hadn't informed them of the color scheme I had chosen. The two of them were clashing with the white, lavender and green beautifying the landscape.

Guests rushed over to greet them as Butch announced their arrival through his P.A. system. I had to give it to Wendell; he looked happy—a lot happier than his new wife did.

Naomi seemed to have an attitude, but I was prepared to ignore that. After all the trouble I had gone through to plan a special event for them, I wasn't about to let her disrespect me with her sour mood.

A small crowd surrounded the newlyweds, and there were a few kids, including mine, running around the yard while Joyce and Naomi's mother chatted near the cake. Everything looked beautiful and was going exactly as planned.

Sweetie's boys were hanging on D.J., Naomi's son, like he was Barry Sanders or somebody, asking him football question after football question. Everyone looked like they were having a good time. There was only one stick in the mud—Sweetie's man, Ric. I guess he wasn't the mingling kind, which meant she would have to babysit him most of the night.

Sweetie walked up behind me. "Everything turned out really nice, Frannie."

"Yeah, it did."

"I put all the food out, but you might want to check and make sure I didn't forget anything," she said, before going over to her man.

Once the bride and groom arrived, the party picked up steam. After the toasts were made, Naomi and Wendell had their first dance, and the party was on.

I was having a great time until I saw Glory walk in the backyard with one of her men. I couldn't believe she had the nerve to show up after leaving us hanging like she did—*yes, I could.*

I went into the house to avoid causing a scene because I really wanted to wring her long, lanky neck. Of course she'd roll in here acting like it was no big deal that she showed up like a guest.

I stood in the dining room window watching her laughing and talking to everybody, introducing her friend who looked young enough to be her son. I was so sick of her shit. She spoke to Naomi and Wendell, and then made her way over to Stephanie, her long lost buddy that I still hadn't gotten the scoop on what Glory had done to run her off.

Michael came up the hallway and saw me standing by the window. "Hey, baby. What you doin' in here?"

"Looking at Glo out there acting like a guest."

"Oh, she finally made it?"

"What do you mean? She was *supposed* to be helping us with this reception."

"Well, we handled everything. Don't trip, Frannie."

"Don't trip? I'm just supposed to act like it don't matter that she didn't help? We don't roll like that in this family."

"Well, just wait 'til later before you say something, alright?"

I walked away from him and went back to the kitchen to busy myself. I would do my best not to create a scene in front of everybody, but I wasn't making any promises.

I looked up and Glory was walking in the house. "Hey Frannie…"

I set down the bowl I was drying. "How you gon' walk yo' ass up in here after everything is done?"

"Everything looks nice. Y'all didn't need my—"

"You weren't even decent enough to let us know you wouldn't be picking up the cake."

"I never said I would—"

"You selfish... self-serving... self-centered... no-man-keeping... bitch." I didn't yell, I didn't scream. Every word I spoke was in an even tone through gritted teeth.

I had cut her down. I could see in her eyes that she hadn't come in expecting to get cussed out, but I couldn't seem to stop myself. I saw a faint hint of defeat in her face, but it only lasted a fleeting moment before she retaliated.

"You think just because you have a husband and can pop babies out left and right, you're unique. Any dog on the street can do that. If you wanna be some man's baby-making machine, that's your life."

That did it. I dove into her and all I could see, besides rhinestones from her top flying everywhere, was the surprise on her face.

Michael appeared out of nowhere and grabbed me, pushing Glory back. He received a couple of blows from both sides for his trouble. Grandma Francine came rushing into the kitchen calling my name.

"Francine! Glo! Stop it!"

We both stepped back, huffing, puffing, and staring at each other.

"Glo, why don't you go back outside—I can't believe the two of you." Michael was pushing me out of the kitchen. We ended up in the powder room under the stairwell.

He locked the door. "What the hell is wrong with you?"

"With me? What about her?"

"You came at her, Frannie. I saw you."

"Did you hear what she called me?" I looked at myself in the mirror. My hair was a little tussled and I was missing an earring, but other than that I looked okay.

"What?"

"A baby-making machine!"

"So what!" He looked at me incredulously. "Have you ever thought that she said it because she doesn't have any children? Why would that make you so mad anyway?"

"You just don't get it." I was still huffing and puffing.

"I don't. And you need to get yourself together so we can go back out there and act like we're hosting this reception."

"Michael, don't blow me off."

"Baby, I'm not blowing you off." He palmed my cheek. "I love you. We can discuss this later. Okay?" Michael smoothed my hair and came in for a kiss. I met him halfway.

We embraced each other, softly at first, kissing in a way that we hadn't in a long time. He pinned me up against the bathroom door, pressing hard into me. Michael raised the hem of my dress and I went for his belt buckle.

"Oh, Francine... I love you."

"I know."

Chapter 26 Joyce

...I wasn't expecting her to let me have it.

"Good morning. I have a ten o'clock appointment with a..." I looked down at the letter even though the name had been embedded in my mind. "... Mr. Imperioli."

Sweetie stood next to me quietly, and I wondered what she was thinking, if anything. Surely, she had no idea how nervous I was.

"Yes, have a seat. I'll let him know you've arrived, Ms. Parker."

The woman at the front desk seemed friendly, and was clearly expecting me. Sweetie and I were dressed in our dignified clothes, ready for whatever. Inside my purse were letters, photos of Carlos and me, and any other proof I could muster up that we had shared a life together.

I kept thinking someone wanted to challenge that Sweetie was his daughter, but if so, then why would they bother us after all this time if we hadn't bothered them? It was all so mysterious. I never sought out Josephine or her children. Nor had I ever mentioned them to Sweetie. I'd been dreading this all weekend long, and now we were about to find out what this was all about.

Several minutes passed according to the huge, old-fashioned clock on the wall. Finally an older lady from behind a set of double doors came out and asked us to follow her.

We followed her into a conference room that could hold about thirty people. I imagined us having to go up against a room full of attorneys, and was wishing I had asked Wendell to come with us.

"Please, have a seat. Mr. Imperioli will be with you momentarily."

The woman closed the door behind her. Sweetie and I sat close together in silence, waiting, which we didn't have to do for long.

"Good morning, Ms. Parker. I'm Mr. Imperioli. Although, you can call me Anthony."

"Good morning, Anthony. This is my daughter, Sanita." I extended my hand to shake his and he lightly took hold, appreciating the fact that I was a lady.

"Good morning, Sanita."

"Hello," Sweetie mumbled.

Anthony was a young Italian man with a long, dark ponytail hanging over the collar of his European suit jacket. His aura was very non-confrontational, so I relaxed a bit. I could tell Sweetie did, too.

"Let me apologize for having to meet with you in this huge room. It was the only one available at the moment."

"Yes, I was wondering how many people would be sitting in on this meeting," I said, exhaling a deep breath.

"It's just us and my assistant, who will be joining us in a moment." I noticed for the first time he was holding two sealed, business-sized envelopes. "While we're waiting for her to bring in the papers, let me go ahead and explain why you're here." He looked at me sternly and continued. "Mrs. Doherty hired us to contact you about some stocks that were owned by the deceased, Carlos Espinoza."

"What type of stocks?"

"It appears that he owned stock in a small clinic that started up over thirty-five years ago, which was later turned into a hospital, before growing into what you may know as Merger Medical Industries."

"Yes, I've heard of Merger."

"Well, as it turns out, Merger Medical is being bought out by Via Christi, and when attempting to contact all original stockholders, the buyout was held up because they were unable to contact the late Dr. Espinoza's family. When they finally reached his wife—or, his wife at the time, Mrs. Doherty, she sold the stock to Via Christi and wanted Dr. Espinoza's child to receive the money." He paused, letting that sink in.

The assistant quietly entered and took a seat next to Anthony, placing what looked like legal forms on the large, oak table.

"So... Why?"

"I'm not sure of all the details, but she has written you a letter..." He held up one envelope. "There is also a cashier's check here for an undisclosed amount for his child, which I'm assuming is you, Sanita?"

"Yes," Sweetie mumbled again.

"It's made out to your mother because we didn't have knowledge of your name." He handed Sweetie the second envelope. "We can reissue it in your name if you wish."

"No. This is fine," Sweetie answered.

Anthony slid both envelopes across the table in our direction. Neither of us reached out to receive them at first, and then I slowly took them in my hand.

"I still have some questions…"

"I don't really know much more than what I've already told you. I'm hoping you'll get your questions answered when you read the letter."

His assistant handed some forms to us, along with a Monte Blanc ink pen. "We just need the two of you to sign at the bottom of both pages stating that you've received both the letter and the check." My mind was going a mile a minute. What was in the letter? And why did Josephine send the money to Sweetie?

I was dying to know what she had to say to me, but the only way I would get my answers was to leave there, and open the envelopes. I signed the first form and passed it to Sweetie.

"What's this second form?"

"It just says that you don't owe us any fees. All fees were paid on the other end… um, by Mrs. Doherty, of course."

I signed the second form and passed it over like the first one. I was anxious to leave but hoped it didn't show.

"I believe this concludes our business. If you should need any assistance with financial planning, we would be happy to make some recommendations."

"Thank you, Anthony. If I should want to contact Mrs. Doherty…"

"She mentioned that everything was in the letter so I would assume that includes any contact information. If that isn't the case, let me know and I will get clearance from her and pass it on to you."

The assistant stacked the papers and stood, prompting us all to stand. We thanked each other, shook hands again, and said our goodbyes. Calmly, Sweetie and I walked out, deep in our respective thoughts.

"Are you okay, Mama?" Sweetie asked when we got inside her car. She was holding her keys and waiting on me to answer.

"Yeah, I'm okay."

She started the car.

"Do you want to go somewhere and open up these envelopes?" I asked, assuming she was as anxious as I was.

"No, I need to get back home. I'll drop you off and you can call me later and let me know what's in there."

"What about the one with the check? You want me to open it now?"

"No. Just wait and tell me later."

"Are you okay, Sweetie?"

"Yeah. I just got some stuff I need to do."

"Okay."

We rode the rest of the way in silence. I did want some privacy to read the letter, but I wasn't expecting her to let me have it. I thought she would be a little more eager to know about the money. But then again, money never motivated Sweetie. Never.

Once I arrived home and changed into comfortable clothes, I slipped on my reading glasses, sat on my bed, and opened the letter.

Dear Joyce,

> *Unexpected as this all must be, I will start by saying that I am contacting you with the best of intentions. I know I can't go back in time and undo the suffering you have undoubtedly endured raising your child alone, but I hope the money will begin to help make up for it.*
> *This is in memory of, and for the love we both have for, Carlos.*

Regards,
Josephine Doherty

I was expecting so much more, but I guess it told me what I needed to know. She was a woman full of regret. The only regret I had was that I didn't try harder that night to make Carlos wait until the morning before heading to Topeka.

I wondered what had given her a change of heart. It didn't matter really, I was just glad she'd reached out, for Sweetie's sake. I laid my head back on the headboard and thought about the beautiful man who had made me so happy. And, as so many times in the past, I began daydreaming about what life could've been like had he lived.

I wiped away the tears that had fallen and then remembered the other envelope. With the same letter opener I made a clean swipe in the top and removed a gray check with blue letters and numbers. "Pay to the order of Joyce Parker." The amount held six zeros following the number sixteen.

It was a good thing I was already laying down or I would have certainly passed out. I continued to look at the numbers. Then I recounted the zeros; and again.

I placed the check back into the envelope, slipped it in my lingerie drawer and broke into a sweat. I called Sweetie on her cell phone and when she didn't answer, I called her home phone. Then I tried her cell again.

Chapter 27 Sweetie

...just a man like every other.

It was the wrong day for Ric to be trippin'. My mother needed me and I was trying to be there for her, but all I could do the whole time we were meeting with the attorney was think about him.

At this juncture, I had a bad understanding of the turmoil Ric was in, but the irrational behavior that showed up without warning left me not knowing how to respond to it. This smooth, together brother who wooed me and knocked me off my feet was anything but. And the episodes were growing worse each time.

Ric spent the previous night sitting in a chair on the other side of the room, calling himself a failure. Once I realized there was nothing I could do to comfort him, I went to bed, but fear that he was going to take off in the middle of the night kept me awake. He never joined me and was in the same foul mood when I woke up.

"Where are you going?" he asked, when he saw me in something other than my usual Tuesday-morning-heading-to-the-shop clothes.

"Remember, I told you I had to go somewhere with my mother."

"Somewhere with your mother, huh?"

"Did you forget?"

"Naw, you just look like you're on your way to meet someone."

"What do you mean?"

He shook his head, staring off into space. "What do you see in me, Sanita?"

"Baby, what are you talking about?"

"Your family is probably wondering why I haven't proposed to you yet."

"No, they're not."

"You deserve a proposal. After your brother's reception the other night... I just can't..."

I could see Ric was really feeling bad. I tried to reassure him. "My family isn't like that."

"You could have any man you want—doctors, lawyers... men who have their shit together. Why are you with me?"

The truth was, with the exception of the current drama, Ric treated me better than any man I had ever been with. He was loving, generous, sweet, and kind. I had never been happier, so it was killing me to watch him go through so much torment. I didn't understand his self-loathing, nor did I know how to address it. I didn't want to mention I was on my way to see an attorney after his comment. So I said nothing.

"I don't deserve you," he mumbled, refusing to look at me.

"Why would you say that?"

"You don't understand it now but the day will come when you'll wonder why you stayed with me. I should save you the trouble and leave now." His voice was calm.

"Are you saying I'm only with you because of your money?"

"What money! I ain't got no money!" He jumped up from the chair and got in my face. "You don't get it, do you? Sanita, I'm busted—broke!"

"So, go and get a job," I said quietly, trying to get him to calm down.

"It's not that fucking simple!" He was still in my face.

I guess it wasn't that simple for a man who hadn't worked a real job pretty much his whole adult life. He didn't know how to go about it and it wasn't my place to help him figure it out. I knew that.

"I'll take care of things until you find something."

"You mean to tell me, when you can have any man you want, you gon' want to be with a man sacking groceries or doing telemarketing?"

Making all of that fast money had given him a false sense of pride which was now destroying his real self-worth. He didn't understand who he was. That he was just a man like every other.

"Maybe you'll have to do something like that at first, but it won't always be that way." I looked at the clock. Damnit, I was going to be late. When I looked back at him, his eyes were heavy with tears.

"Ric, it's going to be okay." I stopped what I was doing to touch his shoulder.

"I'm leaving." A single tear spilled over, rolling down his cheek.

"What do you mean, *leaving?*"

"I'm not gon' drag you and the boys down. I'm leaving." He turned away from me and went to the closet to start packing. I followed him.

"Don't leave, Ric. Everything will be alright." I tugged at his arm but he yanked it away, snatching shirts off their hangers.

"I love you too much to stay."

"Where are you going?"

"I don't know, but I'll figure something out. I can't live here and not have anything to contribute."

"Don't leave right now." I touched his back gently and he seemed to relax a little. "Wait until I get back so we can talk it out."

The phone was ringing and I knew it was Mama making sure I was on my way. She was determined to be early for the appointment. I searched for the phone while trying to watch his every move.

"Hey, Mama. I'm about to walk out... Okay, bye."

Ric was still packing.

"Ric, don't do this right now. I'll be back and we can talk about it then. Everything will be okay. You'll see, baby."

He dropped to his knees right there in the closet and began sobbing like a baby. I rushed to his side and cried with him.

"Please, don't leave, Ric." He stayed there on the floor barely making a sound. "Mama's waiting on me, so I have to go. But, when I get back we'll sit down and figure things out. Okay?"

Ric took in a deep breath, but didn't respond to my plea. I stood, straightened out my clothes, and headed toward the door.

"I'll be right back."

I left, and when I returned, he had packed up most of his things and was gone.

Chapter 28 *Wendell*

...doing a little this and that.

"*... well,* it would've been nice if somebody had asked for my input... Okay! ...at the very least. I know... They threw that reception together so fast; I didn't even get a chance to invite my daddy... Um hmm. And not only do I hate lavender, but I can't stand fruit or strawberries all mixed up in my cake... I can't believe they didn't think to ask what colors I would've liked, or tell us what colors they were going with... girl, I know. It's gon' be a trip being in a family with a bunch of pushy women... like I said, I was blindsided. Before I could mention I was planning my own reception, they had already started putting one together for the day after we got back... his mother? Oh, I don't know, I guess she's okay... but Wendell is her baby for sure... I hope I'm not dealing with a mother-in-law that confuses her son for a husband..."

I had been out for a few hours, doing a little this and that. There was business to take care of at the bank, and I stopped by Naomi's salon to change the filters on the central air unit. I also had clothes at the dry cleaners that were long past needing to be picked up. On the way home I'd gone by Carl's to holler at him because I'd heard that Detra had moved on with her life and gotten married. When I couldn't catch him at home I came on back to the house.

Since I was planning to go back out, I entered through the front door instead of coming in through the garage. Apparently Naomi didn't hear me walk in the house, nor did she notice me standing behind her listening as she dogged out my family.

I slowly moved around the breakfast nook in the kitchen, stepping into her peripheral vision, then moved around until I came face to face with her—mid-sentence. I could tell from the expression on her face that she knew I had been listening long enough to get the gist of her conversation.

"Um hmm... um hmm." Nervously, she continued the call, interjecting affirmations here and there and as I watched her. She glanced up at me periodically, becoming increasingly edgy.

"Hey, let me call you back... Okay, bye."

Naomi placed the cordless phone on the granite countertop and stirred a pot on the stove. "Hey," she said.

She was attempting to blow it off. She closed the lid on one pot and opened another.

"I'm not even gon' ask who you were talking to because I don't give a damn. But, is there anything you want to talk to *me* about?"

"Umm..." Her eyes darted around the room.

"Look—I'm serious about this marriage, Naomi. But if we're gonna make it work, we have to communicate. If you wanted to give your own reception all you had to do was tell me and I could've stopped them."

"I know. I should've said something but it all happened so fast. I didn't know what to do."

"Like saying something to me—or even saying something to them. There were plenty of ways to handle it."

"You're right."

"And regardless of how you feel about my family, you didn't marry them, you married me."

"I know."

"I demand the same respect I give you and in return I expect you to respect them too, the way I respect your family. You don't have to like them."

"It's not that I don't like them," she said, trying to explain. "It's just that... sometimes..." She stopped herself. "I don't know why I said those things."

I wanted to give her a chance to explain, but there was no explanation she could give to make what I'd heard okay.

"Well, what I just walked in on is not the kind of relationship I want with you—you talking about me or my family when I'm not around. That's some shit we' not gon' have."

Naomi didn't say anything. She was normally ready to counter or defend, if not flip a situation entirely, but she wasn't in a position to. Being in the stance of having to be totally apologetic was foreign to her, so she struggled with what to say or do next. I didn't want to shock her system, so I made the next move.

I leaned over, which she wasn't expecting, and kissed her lightly on the forehead.

"I love you," I said, and left the room.

Even though I was angry, I felt it necessary to nip that kind of shit in the bud. We could've argued and made it into a cold war by giving each other the silent treatment, but what would that have accomplished?

One thing I realized was that the success of our marriage largely weighed on my shoulders. My response to whatever problems came up was key. I just didn't expect us to have a situation before the ink was dry on the marriage license. I knew Naomi had a tongue like a razor and was quick to speak with harsh words when she felt threatened by something. I knew her well, and had seen her in action many times.

Besides, most of her insecurities were largely due to my whore-mongering ways, so I felt like I had a lot to make up for. If this was going to work I would have to roll up my sleeves.

Had I approached her differently, she would've felt cornered and been forced to say things she might later regret. It was too hard to come back from those episodes and I didn't want us to have anything hanging over our heads before I went back to Kansas City.

I was tired from all the activities of the past several days so I decided to lie down for a little while. Emptying my pockets, I stretched out across Naomi's bed. I was still having a problem thinking of her possessions as mine, but not necessarily vice versa. I was just nodding off for a nap when my cell phone buzzed and rattled on the nightstand. Joyce's name was on the screen.

"Hey, Joyce."

"Wendell, have you talked to Sweetie today?"

"No, not since the reception. What's the matter?"

"I've been leaving her messages since yesterday and she still hasn't called. And she cancelled her appointments for today."

"Have you called Glo or Frannie?"

"I guess I should. They're both speaking to her even though they're still not speaking to each other. It's just that..."

"Just that what?"

"Well... can you come over here?"

"When? Now?"

"Were you busy?"

"No. I'll be there in a minute."

Joyce wasn't a demanding mother, so I didn't have a problem honoring her request. Usually when she called it was because she needed something done around the house or the salon, and since I would be leaving the next day I needed to go and handle whatever it was.

I slipped back into my shoes, grabbed my keys and phone, and walked back to the kitchen. I was greeted by the smell of something wonderful being prepared. "Smells good in here." I took a sip from the glass of lemonade Naomi had been drinking from. "What are you cooking, my lovely wife?"

"Smothered steak and cabbage. How does that sound?"

"Delicious." The aroma made my stomach growl. "Hey, baby. I'll be back in a bit. My mother called and she needs me to come over."

"Is something wrong?"

"I don't know, she didn't really say what she wanted. I'm assuming she needs me to do something around the house or the shop."

She exhaled heavily. "Don't forget you said you would change the air filters at Black Beauty."

"I already did that."

"Oh." She lowered her eyes. "Thanks, baby."

I lifted her chin and captured her eyes. "Naomi, you are not in competition with my mother, or my sisters."

"I know that."

"I hope so, because I plan to take care of my mother. I won't place her before you, but she will be taken care of."

"I wouldn't expect anything less."

"I'm glad to hear you say that. Come here." I slid my arm around her waist and drew her to me. "The honeymoon ain't over yet, is it?" I kissed her neck, the corner of her cheek bone, and then her lips.

She responded to my touch. "I sure hope not."

"Tell me you love me, girl."

"I love you," she said, between kisses.

"That's what I'm talkin' 'bout. Keep it hot for me, I'll be back."

Chapter 29 *Glory*

...the lingering effect was always worse...

"Your products came today."

"Oh." Frannie had just walked in the door of the salon. "How much were they?"

"I left the ticket on your counter. I believe it was $93 and some change." I continued to work on Gayla, my first client of the day. Frannie and I were the only two scheduled to work.

"Thanks." She reached into her stash and handed me some bills.

I waved her off. "That's okay. I still owed you for those boots you got for me during Von Mauer's last shoe sale."

"They were only $75. I still owe you twenty bucks."

We had our own financial exchange, the three of us girls. Short of kiting checks and currency conversion, the three of us kept each other afloat and thriving by leaning on one another for the bulk of our everyday expenses. Everybody benefited and oddly enough, money was one of the few things we never argued about. None of us cared about coming out even because we learned that if you are waiting to be repaid, as sure as we were members of the Parker family, you would be next to need somebody to have your back.

"Give it to Sweetie," I said. "I owe her for picking me up a blow dryer when mine went out the other day."

"Well, Sweetie owes me, so I guess we're all square."

Just like that, everything between Frannie and me was squashed. As much as we fought, we both hated the silence and tension-filled aftermath of an argument more. It was probably the reason we made up so quickly. We could make each other so mad, but the lingering effect was always worse than whatever the actual fight was about. I guess that's how you do in a family. I was wrong for leaving them hanging with the cake and she was wrong for causing that big ol' ruckus at the reception. I still don't know why my comment about her having a bunch of kids made her so mad. She had the life most single women dreamed of. The whole thing was just so unnecessary.

After the way that evening ended, I didn't expect to hear from RoShon so soon. Part of me was expecting him to play the game and wait the amount of time allotted after sex, or whatever the unwritten rule was, before calling, and the other part wanted to hear his voice again before I got my day started. I was just glad he didn't think my family was demented. After that scene, I imagined him planning to lose my number and forget we'd ever met. He assured me later that he understood all about family drama and then tried to crack a few boxing jokes, calling me Laila Ali.

The scuffle with Frannie notwithstanding, the evening turned out to be one of the best I'd had in a long time. And when he called the next morning, he asked when he could see me again. I guess he's like every other dysfunctional person—attracted and drawn to dysfunction—because any person in their right mind would've let that be the last time they showed their face. His follow-up phone call was sweet and unexpected, just as he didn't expect it when I told him I didn't think things would work out between us.

~~~

Because I'd had a couple of drinks throughout the evening, starting at the restaurant and later at the reception, RoShon insisted on driving me home from Frannie's. I knew he had no intention of coming in, but I had no intention of letting him leave.

"Thanks for seeing me home, RoShon." The two of us stood inside my empty garage after I used the keypad to raise the door. I faced him with my hand gently touching the bulging muscle in his arm. "I would love for you to come in but I know you're only going to reject me if I ask."

"It wouldn't be rejection, Glory. It would be me knowing exactly what would take place if I walked in there," he motioned toward my back door with his head, "and me trying to prevent that from happening."

The diesel engine on his truck was humming so loud the ground was vibrating beneath us. I knew he left it running on purpose, to ensure that he would be getting right back in it. He moved in close, attempting to end the evening with a quick kiss. Taking me by the waist, RoShon brought his face to mine and sweetly kissed me on the lips. I wrapped my arms around his neck, holding eye contact as he moved in, and pressed into him. I could feel his resolve melt away while our tongues mingled. He held on to me a little tighter and kissed me a little deeper.

"Just for a few minutes?" I pleaded once our kiss broke.

I stared into his eyes. He no longer looked like he was considering whether or not to come in. I got the feeling the decision had been made, and he was just trying to make peace with it. We both knew what was next. He released me and quickly moved to his truck, turned off the motor, and engaged the alarm. I closed the garage door and he followed me inside.

I wasn't inebriated enough to miss the fact that RoShon was a world-class lover. He knew his way around a woman's body without question or hesitation. I imagined our lovemaking would be hurried and rushed because of his age, but I was wrong. So wrong. There were no clothes flying off, hard kisses, or exaggerated gestures. It was so slow and good it brought tears to my eyes.

This wasn't what I was used to, therefore I didn't like it. I was prepared for RoShon to follow me to my room, screw me once or twice, and then be on his way before the sun came up. Maybe some dirty words uttered in between thrusts. But in fact, he barely spoke at all, and when he did it was to whisper sweet nothings in my ears while he licked and sucked my earlobes, fingertips, and toes.

While RoShon made love to me, first in the hallway, then in my bedroom, and later in the shower, not one complete, comprehendible sentence left my lips. I had no words. I could barely wrap my mind around what was happening and the sheer *pleasure* I felt. For the first time ever, I had slipped and let myself feel something for a man.

~~~

"This is the second time Marjorie didn't show up for her appointment." Frannie was huffing thirty minutes after her client should've been in her chair.

It was quiet in the shop with the exception of the constant humming of the dryer that my client sat under and some jazz playing on the CD player.

I stacked some Body Glo Pomade on the shelf behind the retail counter. "Hasn't she seen the broken appointment sign on the wall over there?" I was pacing behind the desk.

"Of course she's seen it. She was supposed to be paying a fee when she came in today for the last time she didn't show."

The faded sign had been posted for years, and along with the thirty-dollar fee, it seemed to be a great deterrent for clients not honoring their appointment times.

"Send her a bill and then don't make any more appointments with her," I said.

"I should."

There was nothing like a common interest to seal the reconciliation between feuding sisters. We were all the way back to normal now.

"You've been putting up with her disrespect for years. Missing appointments; running late. And didn't she write you a hot check a time or two? It's time you dropped her ass."

"I know. The only reason I made the appointment to begin with is because she said she knew she owed me thirty dollars for missing her appointment the last time."

"Umm. And now she owes you sixty. How hard can it be to simply cancel an appointment? She clearly doesn't respect your time."

"I think I *will* send her a bill. Where is the letterhead?" She sat behind the receptionist's desk and shuffled through the drawers. "And if she doesn't pay it, at least she won't be making anymore bogus appointments with me." Fueled with revenge or a notion to regain some control, Frannie sat at the computer, and began designing a bill for Marjorie. Since *instigate* is my middle name I was all too happy to put my two-cents in.

"Make sure you let her know you have tried to work with her... and... and you regret the turn in the client-slash-stylist relationship that has occurred... then let her know she will need to take care of the bill ASAP if she wants to do business with you in the future. And then after you get the money, just ignore her ass."

Frannie was pecking away in front of the computer as I recited.

Moments like this are why I could never imagine doing anything other than working with my family. There were so many people who didn't have the support of family the way we did, or couldn't stand being in the presence of their family for more than a few hours. Sure, we had our problems, but we thrived being around each other. That's because of Joyce.

"I'm going up to the house. You need something?" I wanted to see my mother.

"See if Joyce got something sweet…"

When I entered the house, I could hear voices in Joyce's bedroom. I looked through the living room window and saw Wendell's car parked in front. That was odd. I made a beeline for my mother's bedroom and found Joyce and Wendell deep in conversation. When they saw me they stopped talking and tried their best to act normal.

Was there trouble in paradise already? I wouldn't have been a bit surprised with that drama queen, Naomi.

"Hey. What's up?" I asked, plopping down on Joyce's bed.

"Girl, get your butt off my bed. You know how I feel about y'all tracking hair, and God knows what else, into this house."

"Oh, sorry," I said, hopping up.

"Have you talked to Sweetie?" Joyce asked me, as Wendell stood, looking like the cat that swallowed the canary. Something was going down, something big. They clearly weren't prepared to share, but whatever it was wouldn't remain top secret for long. Nothing ever did with the Parkers.

"Un um, not since the other night. Why?"

"I left her a message yesterday and she hasn't called me back. Are you working by yourself today?"

"No. Frannie is there. She wants to know if you have anything sweet."

"I don't know. You can go in the kitchen and look."

"What about the *hair* you don't want me tracking all over the place?"

The phone rang and Sweetie's name and number popped up in big bold lettering on the large dome-shaped, caller ID that Joyce had on her dresser across the room. It was as if she knew she was being summoned.

"There's a cake on the counter. Just take the whole thing over there." Joyce walked to the phone and picked it up.

If that wasn't a dismissal, I didn't know one. Whatever was going on, I could wait to find out about it. "Alright, see y'all later," I said, making my exit.

The last thing I heard was Joyce telling Sweetie that she needed her to come over. The plot was thickening, and I couldn't wait to tell Frannie.

Chapter 30 Frannie

...but something sincere would have been nice.

If only I could rectify things as easily with my husband.

Michael and I tried to have a heart to heart last night. He even asked me if I wanted him to have a vasectomy. That actually got my attention. But was it that simple? I honestly didn't know if my fear of becoming pregnant again was the real reason I didn't want him to touch me. It probably was, but I just wasn't sure.

After our hot moment in the powder room during Wendell's reception Michael thought what was broken had been fixed. Seeing him take charge like he did got me worked up, I guess. The truth was I hated feeling the way I did. Granted, I had been feeling frigid for some time before I was pregnant, and I'm sure the secret I was keeping had to be a factor. What would Michael say if he knew what I'd done? I was sure he'd never look at me the same, but in many ways, I didn't feel like I owed him any explanation whatsoever. Well... I did, but he would've never understood why.

I'd been feeling so overwhelmed. Between work, the kids, my husband, and just being a woman—so much was expected of me. Not to mention the pressures I put on myself, like that damn reception. When Naomi thanked me for hosting it, I got the feeling she didn't mean one word that was coming out of her mouth. I didn't do it to get gratitude from her and Wendell, but something sincere would have been nice.

Glory walked in with Joyce's cake pan while I sat at the desk waiting on my next client. "Here is something chocolate for you," she said, setting the pan in front of me.

"Why did you bring the whole cake?"

"'Cause Joyce was rushing me out of the house; you should've seen them."

"Who?"

"Joyce and Wendell. They're over there acting all strange."

"What's going on?"

"I don't know, but they're looking for Sweetie. Must have something to do with that shady Ric."

"You think so?"

"Probably. Sweetie called when I was leaving but I didn't hear what Joyce said to her. And Wendell was just standing there looking like something big was going down."

"Why do you think it's about Ric?"

"'Cause he's so suspect."

"He *is* that," I agreed. "You would think by now he would be a little more relaxed around us."

"He's shady," Glory surmised, sucking her teeth.

"I think he's just not used to us—he's nervous."

"What the hell is he so nervous for?" Glory asked. "If he was on the up and up he'd have no reason to be nervous."

I washed my hands so I could get into the cake. "True. I just can't see her dating somebody like that."

"Think about it. He has no job to speak of, yet is able to wine and dine her and buy all these fancy gifts. You know that boy ain't legal."

"I hadn't thought about it."

"I bet Wendell found out something about him and told Joyce. That's why they wanna talk to her."

"Could be."

My next client walked in, with Glory's next client right behind her. According to the appointment book we were full the rest of the day.

I loved being at the salon all day and the escape it provided. Until I got home and discovered how much work I *still* had to do at the house. Sometimes I would plop down in a chair after the last client had gone and just... sit there. Glory and Sweetie were always anxious to leave, but I dreaded going home, despite the fact that I loved Michael and the kids. I loved them, I really did. But I hated the amount of energy it took to be with them. There was *always* something to do. I never got a break. There were times when I was fine with the role of wife and mother, and there were even times when I found myself bragging on it. But those days, those moments, were few and far between. As a matter of fact, it'd been an awful long time since I'd felt that way. Something had to change.

Chapter 31 Joyce

After some persistent prodding, the attorney got a message to Josephine that I wanted to speak with her and the day came when she finally got in touch with me. Initially I was anxious to speak to her, but when we actually connected I didn't know what to say.

"Hello, Joyce. This is Josephine." Her voice was exactly as I remembered, calm and mild. The memories flooded my mind, and I felt as though I were back in the little apartment on that awful, dreadful night many years ago.

"I appreciate you getting back to me," I said, and then cleared my throat.

"I take it you got the letter and the check."

"Yes... I—or we did. It was a really nice gesture on your part. The attorney explained everything to me..."

"Well, it was the very least I could do—after all this time."

"But, the amount of the check... I never would've guessed—or expected... What about your own family?"

"My boys are fine. They've had a good life, wanting for nothing." I was trying to get a grasp of her tone. There was a twinge of something nasty there.

"Oh." I wasn't quite sure how to respond. Sweetie hadn't wanted for anything either. I wasn't sure she even missed having a father. Had she known Carlos, she surely would have. But how can you miss what you've never had?

"Joyce, I don't want you to make more of this than what it is. There was money—I knew nothing of it and it belonged to Carlos. I've been remarried for years. It was really the only thing for me to do." She sighed heavily as if she were in pain.

"Not to sound ungrateful, but you really did have other options. We would've never known the difference."

"No, but I would have. It's been hard but I've been trying to let go of some personal things—you know, forgiveness." Her tone was robotic. "I'm not trying to garner sympathy from you but I've been battling cancer for the past eight years—in and out of remission. The cancer is finally winning."

The state of her health came as a shock. "I'm so sorry. I didn't know."

"I only have a couple of months left—if I'm so blessed. It would mean so much to me if you would accept this as a peace offering of sorts."

"I see."

"They don't—my sons..." She paused. I moved the phone closer to my ear.

"Josephine?"

"They don't know anything about your daughter and I would like to keep it that way."

"This is hush money?"

"The money is your daughter's inheritance. Keeping quiet would just be you honoring my request. You haven't said anything all of this time so it shouldn't be that difficult."

The other shoe had dropped.

"Josephine, I was silent all of these years not for your sake and not even for Carlos'. I love my children the same way I assume you love yours. What good would it have done Sanita growing up to know about the circumstances under which she was conceived? But she is a grown woman now and knows the whole truth—how her father loved me and how excited he was about her arrival. If she wants to seek out her brothers I certainly won't try and stop her. If they have character anything like their father's it—"

"Joyce, I didn't call you to rehash the past. Whatever happens, happens. My sons have an untarnished image of their father and if you ever cared about Carlos at all, you wouldn't try and ruin that."

"Well, I feel sorry for you if you believe an image such as his could tarnish so easily."

By the time Josephine and I finished our pointless conversation, I didn't want any part of the money. But what was I to do? Sweetie had made it perfectly clear she didn't want it, and insisted that I take it for all the years of never collecting a dime of child support from any of their fathers. Although I didn't understand why she didn't at least want to split it with me, I respected her decision. But after speaking with Josephine I was rethinking taking any part of the money myself.

I was still trying to relate to Josephine's position. I was never privy to how she may have suffered when Carlos died, and I often wondered if it had been easier losing him in death than it would've been losing him to another woman. I still wanted to understand her pain, even if she never understood mine.

What would Carlos say? What would he want me to do? As I asked the question, my mind went back and I could hear him telling me how he wanted to take care of me, Wendell and Glory. I could hear him apologizing for not doing things the right way, how he would soon make up for it. Was this God's way of finally making an unfortunate situation right? For a long time I was angry with him for leaving me like he did, even though I knew it probably hurt him even more. But that was another lifetime.

So, was I willing to accept the money as something Carlos would want? That was the question.

Chapter 32 *Sweetie*

...the dark abyss that seemed to be awaiting me.

Ric hadn't called. Nor had I seen him despite the fact I had been looking for him for two days. A custom white Hummer would've been hard to miss, so I assumed he'd left town; until I saw someone else driving it.

Eventually I gave up the search and drug myself back to work trying to go on like nothing had changed. But I was lonely and empty. As much as it was killing me, it had to be killing him more. It was easy for me to recognize his attachment to me, but until he was gone I didn't realize how much I was attached to him. I had become dependent upon Ric for so many things.

I did my best to keep it together in front of everyone, waiting until I was alone to fall apart. Sleep refused to come—at night anyway. In bed was where we did most of our talking. Or Ric did the talking and I did the listening. I was not only used to having his body next to mine but I had grown accustomed to his affection. Unlike most men, he loved to touch and cuddle. Without him, the bed was cold. Once he was gone I tried escaping into my reading, which before Ric used to give me so much pleasure, but even that couldn't fill the void. None of the characters in the novels were engaging enough to keep my mind off him.

Maybe something had happened to him. The life he had chosen had consequences, many of them not so pleasant. Was he in prison? Lying in a ditch somewhere? I tried to push the images out of my mind and prayed that wherever he was, he was out of harm's way. Days went by and I was still convinced Ric was going to walk through the door or call one day out of the blue. But it didn't happen. I did the best I could to keep myself from slipping into the dark abyss that always seemed to be awaiting me after a break up.

While waiting on a call from Ric, I noticed how little my phone actually rang, and how often unnecessary calls came in. I figured the more the phone rang, the better the odds were that sooner or later one of those calls would be from him.

The phone rang, and as I was accustomed to doing, I rushed to answer it. My heart sank when I saw Wendell's name on the caller ID. I was tempted not to answer. I didn't want to hear from anyone but Ric.

"Hello," I said, completely deflated.

"What you up to, Sweetie?"

"I'm lying down." Since sleep eluded me at bedtime I had to get it when I could. "What's going on?"

"I'm calling a family meeting."

"I don't think I can make it."

"I haven't even said when."

"Oh. I thought you meant right now. 'Cause I'm resting."

"Naw, I'm not even in town. Tomorrow afternoon at Joyce's"

"What's this about?"

"The money, of course."

"I already said I didn't want it."

"And, ain't nobody trying to make you take it. It's just as well with that thug you got hangin' around."

I was not in the mood to argue about Ric so I held the phone up to my ear not saying a word.

"You need to be there," he insisted.

When Mama told me how much the check was, I could tell she was expecting a very different response from me. And the money did get my attention for a split second. Sixteen million was nothing to sneeze at. But all I could think about was how the money would increase the gulf between Ric and me. It would've totally emasculated him. There was no way he would've been able to handle me having it.

"Are you coming or not?" Wendell repeated.

"Yeah," I said with a yawn. "I'll be there."

Chapter 33 *Wendell*

I so wanted to be her man...

I called a family meeting. Even though Joyce and Sweetie could've cared less about the money, Glory and Frannie needed to know what was up. I had a plan, but it wouldn't be easy to pull off if everybody wasn't on board. I had to be careful with my approach. The human psyche could flip when money came into the picture, and my family was not immune.

I decided not to say anything to Naomi until after all of the Parkers knew what was up. As a husband, it didn't feel right keeping something this big from my wife, but I kept my mouth closed anyway. She and I had enough to deal with without adding another layer to things.

I still couldn't get over all those zeros on the check. I hadn't been able to concentrate on anything else since I found out. I'm sure Naomi could sense something was up, but she didn't push for details. I was thankful for that, as I didn't want to have to lie to her.

Dinner was a haze. The meal I was so looking forward to—I don't even remember tasting it. D.J. ate as if he were in a race trying to get to his homework. He'd rushed in from practice, jumped in the shower, dashed to the table, and inhaled his food. Sydney sat between Naomi and me, playing in her creamed corn. Aside from trying everything to coax her to eat, I sensed Naomi wanted to ask me what Joyce wanted since we had spoken on the phone several times since I'd been back. But she didn't dare.

Later that night, Naomi's mood was sweet and charming. She always got clingy when I made these short trips from K.C. Even though I hated to leave her, I really enjoyed the intimate moments that preceded my departure.

"I love you, baby," Naomi whispered. Our bare bodies were sticky and still touching as we tried to catch our breath.

"I love *you*." I moved her hair and kissed her damp neck a few times.

"What time are you leaving in the morning?"

"I have some things to take care of so I probably won't leave until mid-afternoon." I shifted in the bed and put both arms around her. Our breathing evened out and fell in sync. We were quiet, thinking separate thoughts, but remaining very much connected.

I couldn't help but think about the timing of us getting married and the windfall of money. Would it change things?

I stroked Naomi's back. "Baby, what kind of future do you want?"

"I just want to be happy," she said softly.

"But, what would make you happy?"

"I know exactly what would make me happy." She turned towards me.

"Tell me. I really want to know." We captured each other's gaze.

"The thing that would make me happiest, aside from a healthy family, a long peaceful life, and things like that…" She paused.

"I'm listening."

"It would make me happy if you were good to me."

"Do you have any fears that I won't be?"

She was silent.

"I have every confidence you will be a good husband… *and* father. I hate that it took us so long to get here, but we obviously weren't ready until now. But it's my hope that we'll always feel for each other the way we feel right now."

I raised an eyebrow. "You didn't mention money."

"Money won't make me happy."

"What… did that come out of *my* baby's mouth?"

"Well, money won't make me sad, now…" We laughed a little. "Don't get me wrong, I ain't never mad at money, it just doesn't excite me like it used to."

"Is that right? So, what does excite you?"

"Life itself… and you."

"We excite each other, baby."

Our lips touched and we fell into a silent knowing. Everything would be fine between us because we wanted to make it work. I so wanted to be her man and she, just as much, wanted to be my woman.

Chapter 34 Glory

After an exaggerated delay, and a deep breath...

"I just can't."

"You just can't..." He pondered. "I'm not even sure if I know exactly what it is that you *can't* do."

"I can't do *this*," was all I could say.

RoShon and I had been going back and forth for several minutes as he stood in my doorway spilling his guts. The conversation had gotten off course and he'd lost his train of thought. I added to his confusion by making off the wall comments.

"Okay, again: *this* meaning what?" he asked, his mind in deep disarray. He wanted direct, concrete answers, and I wasn't exactly cooperating.

"*This*, meaning the emotional thing you're needing from me. I can't do it."

"Is that what this is about? Only thing I want from you is your friendship."

"And that's exactly what you have."

"Then why won't you let me come in?"

"If we're really friends I should be able to tell you I don't feel like company right now without you pouting."

"Pouting?" He laughed his signature laugh but unlike before, I was unaffected. "Glory, I can see right through you. You want this. You want this so badly... You just don't believe you deserve good love. This is foreign to you so you shuttin' a brotha down."

"What? What is this some sort of psycho-analysis?"

"I just want to teach you... show you some things."

"You want to *teach* me something?"

"I didn't mean it like that—you didn't let me finish. All I'm sayin' is, the other night scared you. I'm sorry I was so weak and gave in like that. I should've handled myself better and rolled on out, sayin' goodnight at the door."

My face was void of any expression as RoShon ranted on. The things he was saying were so ridiculous I stopped listening

"Look, I won't ask to come in again. I'm gonna leave." Yet he didn't make a move to depart.

"Alright. We'll talk." Abruptly, I closed the door just as he was about to say something else. Relief flooded my whole body and I hoped I'd never see him again. Anybody *that* open and available I just couldn't deal with. RoShon wasn't who I thought he was. He'd disappointed me.

I put my eye up to the peephole and he was still standing there, shaking his head and looking at the door. He reached up to knock again but stopped himself. After watching him for several seconds, I moved away from the foyer leaving him alone with his bewilderment.

My brain switched gears and I prepared myself to go to Joyce's to hear what Wendell had to say. I'd been thinking about it all morning, wondering if he was going to announce he and that she-devil, Naomi were expecting a baby, or something equally ridiculous.

~~~

We all arrived at Joyce's at the same time and took our usual seats around the dining room table.

"So... Why are we here?" I asked. What could be so important for him to drag us over to Joyce's? Anything involving him and Naomi couldn't be of less interest to me.

It was Joyce, Frannie, with Erica sitting on the floor at her feet, and me, scattered around the huge cherry wood table as Wendell leaned against the matching buffet.

"I don't think Sweetie's coming so I may as well get started," Wendell said. He pulled out the chair at the head of the table as though he were going to sit, but didn't. "I have an announcement to make and it's one of those things that I know will drastically change the dynamics of this family. That change can be for good or for bad, depending on how we handle it."

I glanced over at Joyce, who looked as though she already knew what was coming. Frannie was focused in on Wendell, just as I was.

"We've come into some money," he said finally.

"We who?" I asked. My mind went a thousand different directions at once. At first I thought the *we* he meant was he and Naomi.

"This family. The Parkers."

"How much money and from where?" Frannie asked, as her shoulders left the back of her chair.

"It's Sweetie's inheritance from her father," Wendell answered.

The three of us looked over at Joyce. She had been looking down at her hands, which were in her lap. Glancing around the table at all of us, she nodded her head in affirmation.

"How much?" Frannie and I asked together.

"More than enough to do some great things if we use it properly. And I have some ideas."

"You still didn't say how much," Frannie retorted. She and I were on the same page. We weren't trying to move on until we knew exactly what we were working with.

"Sixteen million dollars."

"What!" Frannie slammed her fist on the table.

"Tha hell did you say?" I shouted. "Sorry Joyce…"

"I said, sixteen million," he repeated.

"Oh my God!" Frannie said. She stood and started swinging Ericka around. I joined them.

"Is this for real?" I asked. "Where is Sweetie? Why ain't *she* here?"

"She doesn't want the money, and Joyce said we should use it for the whole family."

"For real? Sixteen million? That's like, what, three point two a piece?" The calculator in my head was not only *dividing* the money, but also *adding up* what I would spend my cut on.

"Both of y'all sit down and shut up," I heard Wendell say.

Frannie and I were busy slapping high-fives and doing the, *we're rich* dance. The way my proverbial checkbook was writing checks, I had spent my millions five or six times over just thinking about trips and shopping sprees.

"This is exactly what I was talking about!" Wendell yelled out and got our attention. "Sit down and let me finish."

We wiggled our fingers, touching the tips, and then obeyed our big brother and sat down.

"Y'all so silly," Joyce said, slowly shaking her head. The money seemed to be no big deal to her and I couldn't figure out why.

"Okay, where did you say Sweetie was?" Frannie asked Wendell. When one of us was missing there was a noticeable imbalance.

"For the last time, I don't know why she's not here," Wendell answered. "When I spoke to her she didn't sound like she would be coming, even though she said she would."

We were curious why Sweetie wasn't there, but it didn't stop us from celebrating. Frannie and I slapped high-fives across the table again.

"Now listen." Wendell got our attention again. "Being the only male in a family full of women has had its challenges, but I wouldn't change it if I could. Joyce," Wendell said, directing his focus to her. "By your example, we learned outstanding work ethics. I don't think any of us would disagree with that. You did a great job raising us by yourself."

Frannie and I obviously needed a moment or two to digest the news because we weren't listening to a damn thing he was saying.

"I believe that we have what it takes right here in this family to create and build a business on a larger scale," he continued. "I've given it some thought, and I have a proposal for you. I hope when we leave here you'll give it some serious thought, maybe even come up with some ideas of your own." Wendell, heavily weighted with authority, gave us his spiel.

Um, I just want my cut, I thought. *Let's just divvy it up.*

Frannie voiced my sentiments. "I think we just need to split it. And if Sweetie don't want her cut, we can split that, too."

"Well, that's not gonna happen," Wendell said.

I spoke up. "Why not? I'm sure Naomi would be happy to get her hands on some money."

"Glory, shut up," Wendell said calmly.

"Don't tell me to shut up!"

"If you were saying anything worth listening to, I wouldn't."

"Glo, let him finish," Joyce said.

After an exaggerated delay and a deep sigh, Wendell continued.

"Having a chain of cosmetology schools would be a great business venture. But that's *my* dream and I don't think the rest of you have a burning desire to teach or be involved in cosmetology education. And that's okay." He looked around the table. "What I propose is that we take two percent of the money to invest in one of our dreams and I think it should be Body Glo. I believe if we all got behind it and helped Glory develop and sell her products, eventually we could be bigger than Bronner Brothers."

Now he had my attention. Yeah, I was tripping thinking about houses, cars and trips to Africa.

"We'll get a financial advisor—"

"Financial advisor? Don't you have to pay them? There goes the money." I sucked my teeth.

"Glo, don't be ignorant. No one will have free reign over the money, including you, that is, *if* everybody agrees on investing in Body Glo."

"What about the rest of the money?" Frannie asked.

"It will sit in an account and at some point maybe we'll invest some or put some in a Roth account. No one will be able to use it for personal reasons. We'll give Body Glo, or whatever we decide to invest in, three to five years to turn a profit. Then we'll decide if we want to expand it or go on to invest in the next idea."

"That sounds really good, Wendell," Joyce said.

"So, how is that going to benefit everybody?" Frannie was starting to have that jealous tone in her voice, like nobody would let her sing the lead all over again.

"We will *all* own shares in the company, and we will *all* work in the business in some capacity."

"What about tithes? You haven't mentioned paying tithes on the money. We need to do that if we want God to bless what we do with it," Frannie said, knowing she wouldn't have been thinking about tithes if we were talking about investing in one of her ideas—which she had none of.

"I haven't said anything about paying taxes on it either," Wendell said matter of fact. "There are a lot of things to discuss and we're not making a move until we do."

My mind opened up. I could see Body Glo products on the shelf of any and every store that carried cosmetics or hair care products from coast to coast. Just that quick, I lost my appetite for weeklong spa retreats and clothes and shoes from the finest stores. I felt a little foolish for allowing my mind to diverge into a state of ghetto ignorance instead of first thinking about the opportunity we had to grow sixteen million into a hundred million. I understood what Wendell was trying to say. The Parkers had arrived.

Chapter 35 *Joyce*

...just a few stumbling blocks.

Bronze and white cases lined every wall of the building, on shelves or piled high from the concrete floors to the open ceiling. After hiring a couple of chemists to improve the shelf life, the overall usability of the products, and creating new bottles and jars, there were stacks and stacks of boxes waiting to be shipped out to fifteen different states. A couple of setbacks slowed things down, like needing to change packing companies a few times and not knowing to print *Shake Well* on the bottles of dandruff shampoos where emulsion was an issue. But in the bigger picture, these were just a few stumbling blocks. And yet, we still had a lot to learn.

The warehouse we'd purchased was on the east side of town and according to Wendell, we'd gotten a great deal on it and bought it outright. It was enjoyable to be doing something other than standing behind the hydraulic chair and even more so to be doing it alongside my children.

Wendell and Frannie were in charge of business operations and sales. They both had a real knack for negotiating sales and handling the paperwork and business side. Sweetie and I work the graphics department, along with a professional of course, designing images for the literature, labels, bottles, and jars. We've had the best time working together and it seems to have pulled her out of her once-again heartbreak slump. This has definitely been a welcome distraction for her.

Glory was working every department along with working everybody's nerves but we were happy to overlook her for the success of the business. She has taken leave from doing hair, which keeps Sweetie and Frannie hopping, doing her clients along with their own. But they aren't complaining about that either.

Life seems to be moving right along for everyone. Wendell is busier now than he's ever been balancing and maintaining a marriage, family life, and two demanding businesses.

Frannie even seems to have a new purpose in life and is less grumpy about her role as wife and mother. Maybe the answer for her was to simply get out of the house more. I really don't know. I've wanted to ask her about the pregnancy I saw in her face that day, but I'm sure that it's better that I don't.

Love will keep us going just as it always has…

BOOK CLUB GUIDE

1. Would you consider the Parkers a dysfunctional family? Why or why not?
2. Are some of the Parker family issues representative of the issues in your family or families you know? How or how not?
3. What kind of a mother do you consider Joyce Parker to be?
4. Which lifestyle do you think has had the greater impact on the sisters' lives and how they handle their relationships—Joyce's or Wendell's? Why?
5. What kind of a man do you believe Wendell to be?
6. Based on Wendell's past womanizing ways, do you think his marriage will last with Naomi?
7. What is Glory's real issue with men and why can't she connect with them?
8. Should Sweetie have tried harder to help Rick through his hustler's withdrawal or ran at the first sign of him having an addiction problem?
9. Was Frannie's real fear of intimacy with Michael because of a fear of becoming pregnant or just a typical female habit of never being satisfied with what she has? Why?
10. Will the windfall of money be a blessing or a curse to the Parker family?